NO BRAKES PUBLISHING Presents...

Natural Born Killaz

Terry L. Wroten

Sale of this book without a front cover may be unauthorized. If this book is coverless, it may have been reported to the publisher as "unsold or destroyed" and neither the author nor the publisher may have received payment for it.

Copyright © 2010 by Terry Wroten

Published in the United States
ISBN 978-0-9834573-2-9

All rights reserved. Except as permitted under the Copyright Act of 1976, no part of this publication may be reproduced, distributed or transmitted in any form or by any means, or stored in a database or retrieval system, without the prior written permission. Please do not participate or encourage piracy of copyright materials in violation of the author's rights. Purchase only authorized editions.

This is a work of fiction. Names, character, places, and incidents either are the product of the author's imagination or are used fictitiously. Any resemblance to actual persons, living or dead, events, or locales is entirely coincidental and not intended by the author.

Book edited by Zakiyyah Denton
Book cover designed by Baja Ukewli
Interior Book Designed by Lishone' Bowsky

Dedicated to my Granny Faye Ella Woods and my aunt Cassandra Woods. Rest in Peace.
Also to Decap and Scrappy Loc, y'all was my real homies who saw my talent before I did and told me to make it out of the hood. Damn, I wish y'all were here to see my dream become reality. Love y'all!"

TABLE OF CONTENTS

CHAPTER 1.
11

CHAPTER 2
19

CHAPTER 3
37

CHAPTER 4
47

CHAPTER 5
69

CHAPTER 6
81

CHAPTER 7
85

CHAPTER 8
93

CHAPTER 9
103

CHAPTER 10
117

CHAPTER 11
123

CHAPTER 12
135

CHAPTER 13
147

CHAPTER 14
155

CHAPTER 15
159

CHAPTER 16
165

CHAPTER 17

171

CHAPTER 18

183

CHAPTER 19

197

CHAPTER 20

209

EPILOGUE

219

ACKNOWLEDGEMENTS

223

CHAPTER 1

Sunday, February 6th, 2005

Dead man walking, dead man walking," the guard shouted as he escorted his prisoner down the piss yellow corridor. He yelled it every time they passed a security gate en route to the visiting room. His partner slowly brought up the rear with his baton at the ready, incase he had to do some skull cracking. Both men were dressed in heavy flack jackets and helmets with metal visors.

The young man shuffling between them didn't look to be more than a teenager, but the glint in his eyes portrayed a far older soul. They were the eyes of a man who had seen too much too soon. Cold iron shackles snaked his wrists and waist, with an additional length of chain that went to his ankles. The chains made it almost impossible to move, so he shuffle-waddled to try to keep in step with the guards. The excessive restraints seemed a bit extreme, but the guards knew better than to take unnecessary chances with one of L.A.'s most notorious gang members, Killa Black.

The guards shoved him into a small stall which contained a small desk with a small metal stool attached to it. A thick Plexiglas divided the room but there was a phone box mounted next to the glass so that the inmates and visitors could communicate.

Being denied physical contact with his visitors irritated Killa Black, but he tried not to complain about it. This was understandable considering the circumstances surrounding him being in prison in the first place. He was happy just to see a face that didn't hate him.

When the steel door slammed behind him, KB pressed his body against it so the guard could reach through the slot and undo the shackles that bound his wrists to his waist. It was no accident when the guard jabbed the key roughly into his stomach in the process of unlocking the shackles, but Killa Black managed to suppress the urge to try and break the guard's hands. When he was free of the chains, KB sat down on the stool and patiently waited for his visitors.

Over the last few weeks, he had rejected several visits—mostly from journalists who wanted to ask him dumb ass questions. In their eyes they didn't see John, a young man who allowed his environment to force him into some very poor choices. Instead, they saw Killa Black, the man who stirred hundreds of Crips to wash the ghettos of Los Angeles in blood. To them, he was a dollar sign and a ratings booster. When he was on the streets Killa Black had been the king of his castle. He had a queen and pawns, but he was so caught up in the streets he didn't realize what he had or who he was—until a man Killa Black had never seen or done wrong sentenced him to death.

~~~~~~

KB smiled when he saw the group of friendly faces cram into the visiting area. Leading the pack were his mother and his sister Jasmine, who he hadn't seen in months. Also on the visit were his nephew, sister in-law, his son's mother and most importantly his baby boy Don. Tears almost welled in his eyes at the sight of his son, the only thing good he ever brought into the world. Keeping his emotions in check, Killa Black kept smiling and greeted his family.

TERRY WROTEN

His mother was the first visitor to sit down and pick up the plastic phone. "Hi John, how are you?" She was getting up in age, but was still a very pretty woman. You could see the worry lines that he had created in the corners of her eyes and around her lips, but her eyes were still bright and hopeful. To his mother he was still John, but it didn't take a rocket scientist to see what Killa Black had put her through.

"I'm doing fine. What about yourself?" her son replied.

"I'm doing fine," she informed. "I'm glad to see you're still holding it together, considering what's going on," she seemed tired when she spoke. "It seems like everytime I turn around someone else's child is condemned to this madness. I don't know when young Black men are gonna learn and understand that we are helping *them* win the war by putting ourselves into these kinds of situations. They say that prison is supposed to rehabilitate you, but these jails aint nothing but a modern day Auschwitz."

His mother had to have been in one of her moods because she was going in on him. Killa Black learned from his oldest brother Benjamin, who was now living in Cuba, why Mama was so radical against the White man. Back in the day, she had been a member of the Black Panther Party and a firm supporter in the movement, created to re-educate young African Americans. Benjamin had heard several stories from his sources about his mother's exploits, and was proud to have come from such a down sister.

"Okay, I know... I'm talking too much," his mother said, reading his face. "But while I'm thinking about it, you know those White people have been calling the house everyday to interview me about you? It seems like everybody with a television show, magazine, or radio station wants to hear from the woman who birthed one of America's worse nightmares," she half joked.

NATURAL BORN KILLAZ

"Mama, you aint gotta talk to them people."

"I know, but I get a kick out of it. I always tell them what they don't want to hear," she laughed. "These folks must be crazy if they think I'm gonna buy into all that bull they spewing. The media don't know my son, and I set them straight everytime."

"Right on, Mama," he smiled.

"You know I keep it gangsta. But the other day I got a call from a woman named Barbara and her husband Terry about something that may interest you."

Killa Black searched his memory bank. "You mean the lil homey from the Eastside?" KB asked surprised. He knew Terry from when he was on the streets doing dirt and had heard about his efforts to get out of the life but hadn't kept much track of his progress.

"Yes, the same one. He put down his flag and picked up a pen, thank God." She raised her hand for emphasis. "Terry has got a real gift and he wants to pen a book and make a movie about you. John, I know how you feel about people trying to exploit you and your situation, but I've got a good feeling that Barbara, you, and Terry are cut from the very similar cloths. I believe in what he's trying to do. Who knows, if the two of you can get together and raise the right kinda noise, then we might even be able to cheat the devil outta my baby."

Killa Black pondered it. His lawyer Jay Cooper had been making some positive strides with his appeal but still hadn't quite gotten the push where a judge would agree to hear it. An additional resource was just one more bullet in the chamber and Killa Black needed a full clip if he stood any kind of chance to win the battle ahead of him.

"John," his mother continued, "These people have quite a bit of power in the community, and have come up with a way to spin your story into something positive. Barbara wants to publish it and split the proceeds between your appeal costs and a program they started called Save Our Kids. It's a non-profit organization that reaches out to kids in the hood and helps them to make the transition out of the gang life and way of thinking. Her husband thinks that he can pen your story in a way to make these kids understand the hell that comes from this ignorance."

KB just regarded his mother curiously. He wasn't used to his mother vouching for anyone that she didn't push out of her own womb, so the fact that she was campaigning so hard for Terry and Barbra made him wonder.

"John, I know how you feel about your circumstances and the picture they've painted against you, but you've got to put your bitterness to the side for a minute and think about the next generation. Them boys ain't gonna know the tragedy of your life, but the legend of exploits and they're gonna line up by the hundreds to walk in your shoes, unless you do something to try and change that. Your Daddy, bless his soul, fought hard for what he believed in and for as much as I hate to admit it... you did too," she said with distain in her voice. But the difference between you two was what you were fighting for wasn't something positive."

"Yeah," Killa Black said dryly.

"John, you better look at the writing on the wall. You're in here fighting for your life, and the bullshit war that put you here is still going on. The racist cops are still locking kids up in our neighborhood and people are still getting killed. Can you honestly say your sacrifice changed anything? Of all your friends, Rat is the only one doing any good and staying out of trouble and still keeping in contact. I love him like a son because he's been a *real* friend to you."

NATURAL BORN KILLAZ

John agreed. Rat had been the only one out of all his so-called homeys to keep it real since his incarceration. Truth be told, Rat was also the only one out of his crew that escaped prison, death, and had made it out of the hood. Mama rambled on another journey of words about Rat without even noticing and KB gave Jazz the nod to get on the phone. There was only 15 minutes left of visiting time and he wanted to make the rounds.

Jazz was a UCLA graduate and the brains of the family, as well as a blessing to have as a sister. While everybody was getting caught up, Jazz kept her head down and did what she had to do, refusing to become a statistic of the hood. From the time they were kids, she had always been the rock of the family and as a woman became its backbone.

"Hey, Black Boy!" Jazz smiled.

"What it do?" KB chuckled.

"I miss you," she said, touching the glass. "I talked to Benjamin the other day and he said to tell you to stay strong."

Killa Black nodded.

"Well, we don't have much time, so I will get straight to the point. John, I came all the way up here with everyone else to talk you into agreeing on allowing Barbara and Terry to do this. It will truly help kids growing up in the socially deprived inner cities, or should I say the 'hood'?"

Killa Black smirked at her. "Jazz, you and Mama in here going all around the bush for some nigga y'all don't even know like that to say if he's a real writer. I've read books by Terry McMillan and Teri Woods but never a Terry Wroten."

"He's a friend of mine. Barbara and I were roommates around the time she met him and I used to always say how much he reminded me of you," Jazz explained.

TERRY WROTEN

"There's only one Killa Black," he checked her.

"Yeah, but there's thousands of dedicated Crips all across the country, so none of you are really more than just cogs in a big wheel," she shot back. "Anyway, Terry used to be a knucklehead too but he's pulling his life together real nice. When I told him that you were my brother we got to talking and... you know the rest. I've read his stuff John, it's really good."

"I don't know about all this, Jazz," he grumbled.

"I can understand that. Just promise me you'll at least think about it?" "A'ight."

"Good, I gave Terry your mailing address so you should be getting a letter from him soon."

KB sat there with his arms folded looking at his sister through the plastic divider. Something about the situation sat funny in the pit of his gut. "A'ight Jazz, what's in it for you?"

"John, who said there was something in it for me?"

He just started blankly at her. Jazz sucked her teeth. "If you must know, I will be getting a finder's fee for making the introduction and consulting on the project."

All John could do was laugh because he knew his sister oh so well. Jazz had probably worked out all the details including the speech before she even decided to come up and see him about the project. "Jazz, you're the smartest snake I know." He gave her a mischievous grin that she hadn't seen since they were kids.

"So I take that as a yes?" she asked anxiously, but before her brother could answer the visit was over.

"Inmate Wilson, your time is up!" The guard banged on the steel door.

KB raised his finger asking for one more minute. "Jazz, I gotta think about it. If I get a letter from Terry, me and him can kick it but don't get your hopes up."

NATURAL BORN KILLAZ

Jazz rolled her eyes. "Well... it's better than no."

"Wilson, don't make me call you again," the guard threatened. Jazz was about to snap, but Meosha beat her to it.

"Fat boy, you need to calm yo' 15 dollar an hour ass down before you
get the shit slapped out you when you get off work!" She rolled her neck. Killa Black doubled over in laughter. Meosha was ghetto-fied. She'd
been ghetto her whole life, and that mouth of hers was something else. "Me-Me, let's not get ghetto in here," Jazz pinched her thigh.

The whole exchange made John smile. Awhile back he would've scoffed at the catty drama, but as he drew closer to his day of judgment the smallest things like a family argument seemed more precious than they had been before.

The family said their goodbyes and John was re-shackled and led back to his block. Sleep didn't come easy that night, as he lay awake thinking over his life. Some time around midnight, he fell into deep thought and found himself reminiscing.

CHAPTER 2

Thursday, February 10th, 1994

Carver Middle School is where Killa Black got his name and learned the game. Carver was the junior high school every popular teenager in South Central went to, or tried to be enrolled at. It was on the Eastside of town and directly around the corner from Killa Black's house. It was the only predominantly Black school left in Los Angeles. The Mexicans were starting to out number Blacks, 3 to 1, in every other school. Carver had a White principal named Mr. Ruby, who went along with any and everything, as long as he got his salary and the school was running alright. Which meant, no gang fights or riots.

The year was 1994 and Hip-Hop was becoming nationally known. Since Carver was considered an all Black school, Mr. Ruby organized Black DJs from around the way to come spin a few albums in the school gym every Friday. To the students, the gym was like a house party on Fridays; and this was the way that Mr. Ruby kept the peace. Homeroom at Carver was Killa Black's favorite class. Miss Phillips, a black woman and his homeroom teacher, was no older than thirty-five and looked more like a student than a teacher. She was a hip Afro-centric woman. Her class was filled with art, ornaments, and wooden sculptures. Everything in that class equaled red, black, and green.

Miss Phillips was extremely into her Blackness and knew the struggle kids in Los Angeles went through; especially with the

NATURAL BORN KILLAZ

gang culture of the Crips and Bloods. When it came to Killa Black and his crew of wannabe-Crips, she vowed to herself to lead them straight. Miss Phillips knew most of her students were born to ride for the cause of either the Red or the Blue. She attempted to talk to John about the destructions of the Black man but he told her straight out, "I hear enough of that talk from Mama, and I don't need to worry about red, black, or green when I'm true Blue."

After the talk with Miss Phillips about what he wanted to do with his life, Killa Black strutted out of her class. Miss Phillip was heated. John had so much potential, the boy could have easily been a doctor, lawyer, judge or someone special. But sad to say, for young John, it was Crip or nothing! And he told her exactly how he felt, "This Crip here!"

Miss Phillips screwed her face, stunned. Tears filled her eyes. She sensed she was about to lose another one of her students. He was at the mouth of the beast, the streets, and the beast was going to eat John alive. Miss Phillips just knew it, but she couldn't quit. She felt with a little more guidance he could have made the right decisions, which would have put him on the right path in life.

"Well, if I can't get to you, you give me no other choice but to call your mother. John you are too smart to let this Blue stuff around here bring you down."

Killa Black was a full fledged wannabe at this time, and no one the universe could have challenged or changed his mind about becoming a high ranking Crip in the Crip organization.

He snarled, "I don't care! This Crip here! This Crip here!! This Crip here!!!"

Killa Black was so stuck on being a Crip, he could care less who didn't like it.

After Miss Phillips called his mother, Mama placed him on punishment for a month. But being on punishment didn't change anything and somewhat hardened John. Eventually Miss Phillips had no choice but to accept John as a wannabe. Besidse from being his homeroom teacher, she could relate to the inner conflict he was going through. Miss Phillips had actually ran with the Crips in her younger days. Being born and raised in L.A., before going to Cheyney State and turning Pro-Black, she established a name for herself in the Crip community. In addition to that, Miss Philliphs had reputable gang members in her family.

One day, holding up a pair of Afro-Centric ornaments and a pair of wooden sculptures, Miss Phillips smiled at John and said, "John, I'm asking the spirits of our ancestors to give me the strength to express my troubles to you."

"Troubles?" He looked at Miss Phillips with suspicion. John wasn't trying to hear no political speeches. Mama gave them everyday and he wasn't about to sit and listen, especially since it was nutrition break and Miss Phillips was taking away from his free time.

"You want to go to nutrition and hang out with your little crew, huh? I know your boys are more important than me, but John can I have five minutes of your time? Better yet, let me rephrase that, Mr. John 'The Black Giant' Wilson, can I please have five minutes of your time?"

John started chuckling. Miss Phillips knew everything that went on around school and actually took pride in knowing it. Truth be told, Miss Phillphs should have been the principal, because Mr. Ruby didn't care about nobody or nothing, especially if it didn't concern him. Miss Phillips stayed in the mix. She also stayed trying to lead John and his friends the right way, but they were only interested in doing their own thing. The Crip thang.

"Black, what's so funny?" she asked.

It brought a smile to John's face knowing that Miss Phillips knew his nickname. John was the biggest student at Carver and stand-

NATURAL BORN KILLAZ

ing six foot two. He was fourteen and a giant amongst the other students. John weighed about two hundred and ten pounds solid. He was so big to his peers they called him, 'The Black Giant'. John's dark complexion had always been the color purple, so he took the name and ran with it.

He looked at Miss Phillips and said, "I'm laughing because I'm wondering how you know about my nickname?"

Miss Phillips shook her head as if saying, "boy you just don't know". Miss Phillips pulled out a chair and sat right next to him, "John, that's what I want to talk to you about. I know more than you think. I know your name is Black, Kevin Goodman's name is Kev, and he's your best friend. I know that Wesley Jake's name is Big Head. Michael Brown's name is Money Mike or Money. Nathan Williams is Little Loco and that's your whole crew!"

John was busted. She knew everything! He cracked a one-sided smile and laughed it off.

"You know what I also know?" Miss Phillips continued. "I know that you and half the brothers in this school have a crush on that little girl Donita Jackson!"

John always had a crush on Donita and it started right there in Miss Phillips' class. Donita was the youngest and prettiest ninth grader in school. She was thirteen and very popular, she stood five two with hazel cat eyes, a light complexion, and long hair. Donita Jackson was his whole crew's dream girl. They fought over her everyday!

"Miss Phillips, how do you know so much? I thought you were too heavy into your Blackness to know that!"

Miss Phillips shook her head again with that same "boy you just don't know" look and said, "I wasn't born yesterday. I grew up in the hood too. I grew up on the Westside. I got family who's living that crazy life, and they're not wannabes." She rolled her eyes

TERRY WROTEN

matter of factly.

John was surprised to hear some of the things his teacher was saying. He didn't know that she wasn't always Pro-Black. They eventually talked through that whole nutrition break. At lunch, he went back to her class. She was cool after all. John figured, if she wasn't talking that Black political stuff, and wasn't telling him what he should or shouldn't do, he was all game. When the bell that signaled the end of lunch rang, he told her he'd talk to her later.

The last school bell rang at 3:20 pm. After leaving class, John stood in the front parking lot, awaiting his crew. His crew consisted of everyone Miss Phillips named: his best friend Kev, Money Mike, Big Head, Little Loco, and himself. They were five little wannabes, but had Carver on lock. They were all claiming Crips, like they were true members. They had the whole school under their spell. They met in the school's parking lot after school every day, before walking to Jack-In-The-Box and Kev's house. Kev's house and Jack-In-The-Crack, as they called the famous restaurant, were their after-school-hangouts. These were the spots where they loitered and banged Crips. However, the only real Crips were their brothers, cousins, and family members.

When the five man crew was accounted for, they mobbed to Jack-In-The-Crack. It was right up the block on Vernon and Central. That day, before the crew left the school's parking lot, John spotted Miss Phillips standing at the entrance of the school nodding her head at him in a disgusted manner. He looked at the ground after eye contact was made. Miss Phillips was hurt. She really cared and wanted to say something, but she knew from their talks that John was already too far gone. In the gang culture, you could just look at a wannabe and tell if he really wanted to be a gangster, or if he was just going through an identity crisis John and his crew had their minds made up, they were gangsters.

NATURAL BORN KILLAZ

Seeing his teacher, John pulled up his blue Dickies that were sagging below his waist and waved at her. Miss Phillips had earned his respect as a teacher; and as a fine Black teacher from the hood!

"Cuzz why that bitch Miss Phillips always watchin' er'thing we do?" Kev asked.

John smirked while replaying the conversation he had with Miss Phillips during nutrition. Kev had no idea Miss Phillips was from the hood. John wanted to tell him, but he decided against doing so in front of the whole crew. Miss Phillips asked him not to tell anyone in his crew about her past, but Kev was John's best friend. They never kept anything from each other, and John wasn't about to start making changes.

"Cuzz, Miss Phillips is cool," John hintedly informed. "Don't trip on her. She's good. I got the 4-1-1 on her. I'll tell you later."

"Naw nigga tell me now," Kev demanded.

John declined. The word "Cuz" was used regularly. It was part of their Crip-lingo. The N word, B word, and MF word were also used in regular conversations. Ebonics and degrading words were their way of talking. It was no doubt they were hood orientated and degrading to themselves, but no one ever paid any mind to how they talked, for it was how they lived.

John didn't want to keep talking about Miss Phillips, so he changed the subject.

"Cuzz, I don't care about Miss Phillips, but I know imma make Donita my girl!"

Money Mike did a military stop on the dime when he heard Donita's name. "Cuzz, whacha say?"

"Nigga, you heard what I said."

"Put that on something," Money Mike said staring at John.

John screwed his face. "Nigga, that's on my mama."

At that point Kev chimed in. "Cuzz don't be puttin that on Miss

TERRY WROTEN

Wilson, fool."

John laughed. "Ha!" His whole crew waved him off. He told them to trust in his player-ism. "Imma Crip, nigga!"

Kev smacked his lips, "Is that right?"

"What you doubtin' me?"

"Yep. Nigga, seal the deal. You hard." Kev was telling John to put that on Crip. He was trying to pull John's bluff in front of all the homies. Everyone had stopped walking and all eyes were on them. The crew knew that the conversation was getting heated and wanted to see if I John was going to seal the deal.

John had confidence in his game. He was a fly, handsome, young guy, so he had to seal the deal and come up with a plan. He countered, "On Crip."

Kev shook his head and started cracking his knuckles. "Nigga, you betta hope and pray she give you some play. If not yo' ass is grass!" Kev stood five foot and was very active. He was like a little Pit Bull Terrier. He had a little man's complex and was easily offended. He loved fighting and was good at throwing blows. His brother Crip Van and John's brothers were the leaders of the Eastside Crips. Kev and John lived next door to each other and had been best friends since birth. They considered themselves brothers.

John countered Kev's threat and said, "Cuzz, I'm not worryin' 'bout my ass being grass or gettin' discipline..."

"Hol' up!" "Hol' up!!" Mike yelled cutting John off before he could finish his sentence. He then got on Kev, "Kev you always tryna get somebody disciplined. Nigga you aint no big homie, so wontchu stop tryna act like Killa or somebody fool." Mike's sarcasm and taunting caused Kev to become irate. However, Money Mike cared less about Kev's heated temper.

"Kev, you swear every bitch in school likes you. Nigga, just because you fucked ol' hoodrat ass Candy, don't think all these other bitches in the school like you. I'll get Donita before you. And that's on Crip, nigga."

"Mike, aint nobody talkin' to ya bitch ass so cuz, mind yo' business," Kev snapped. He had a strong belief if you were speaking your mind with him, and you two were not in agreeance with each other, you were speaking against him.

Mike was no where near a bitch; his status amongst the crew was vicious. He was a True Gansta and true figure in the crew. To most, he resembled Snoop Dogg. He was slim, with long hair, and considered himself a player. Niggas around the block called Little Loco, Big Head, and Mike, "Tha Dogg Pound." He looked so much like Snoop Dogg. Little Loco looked like Kurupt. And Big Head looked like Daz, except with a bigger head.

Mike glanced at John and frowned. His frown read, "Did cuzz just call me a bitch?'

John tooted his lips up and furred his brows, "Yep he did just that."

Mike snarled. "Nigga, you'sa bitch!"

Kev gave Mike the evil eye and snarled back, "You the one gettin' mad over a joke, so you'sa bitch. Bitch!"

John, Big Head, and Little Loco started instigating. The crew were all known to instigate fights between each other; and truth be told, they all had hands like Zab Judah due to fighting each other. It didn't take long before the trio encouraging "ow's" and "argh's," had Mike and Kev in an alley next to Jack-In-A-Crack, squaring off for battle.

John screwed his face for instigating a fight between two of his good friends. He wouldn't have normally allowed Kev to fight by himself, however, Mike was a homie too; so he had to let them fight it out pound for pound like Sugar Ray and Duran. When they got tired, the trio combine tried to break it up, but Kev and

TERRY WROTEN

Mike wanted to keep going. Mike had Kev by atleast seven inches, but Kev was staying with him. They went at it like cats and dogs. No one could claim a victory so John stepped between them to break it up once again.

"A'ight! Cuzz, that's enough!"

Kev wasn't about to give up or show any signs of weakness. He said agitated "Cuzz, watch out!"

"Move!" Mike yelled at John.

John stepped from between them and they were at it again! This fight was based on pride so these two wannabes were going to fight their hearts out. After it was over, they were mad at each other no longer than two hours. Once they hit the block, they were back buddies. In the crew, they were used to getting into fights one minute and then back to boys the next. What made it even worst, they were really just training each other for future battles with the rivals, The Bloods.

At this point in time, the rivals weren't the Bloods. The enemies were the older Crips. There was a tradition that the older Crips gang up against the younger recruits or wannabes every so often. It was the old versus the young, so fighting amongst themselves was the best training. In the hood, you had to know how to fight, because the vultures prey on the weak. The jungle creed must feed.

"Cuzz, what it is?" John's oldest brother Killa asked his crew when they made it to the block. It was obvious that Mike and Kev had come to some grief. "I guess, you niggaz been gettin' into it huh? So what's the biz?"

Benjamin, or Killa as he was called on the streets, was the leader of the Eastside Crips. Killa was twenty-two and hood rich. He stood about three inches taller than John. They looked very alike, almost like twins, from head to toe. John looked up to his older brother. Killa was his idol. John's other brother Loco was second in com-

NATURAL BORN KILLAZ

mand. He was eighteen. Loco had as much money as Killa and he owned a Mercedes Benz, a S500 on rims! Loco and Jasmine were close and had a brother-sister bond that was unbreakable. Jasmine was seventeen and Loco spoiled her. John envied the way Loco treated their sister. But he was lucky. He was the baby. Killa and Mama spoiled him with everything.

John's family was known on the Eastside as Drug Lords and Gantsta Crips. So when Killa asked "what it is?" the crew told him everything. On the streets of Los Scanless (Los Angeles), Killa was the truth. He was prayed to like God by most Crips.

The wannabes said in unison, "This Crip shit is the biz and we gettin' ready fo' any nigga who try to test. Nahmean?"

After the young crew reported to Killa, he looked at them and nodded. Mama and Kev's mother, Miss Goodman, didn't get off work until five, or sometimes six when they worked overtime, so both houses were hangouts until then. When Mama was on her way home, John would run into the house and clean up. This was because he had to make it look like he'd been home, instead of hanging out claiming Crips.

After school, the next day, the crew did their usual before heading to John's house. "Ay, cuzz no hangin' out today," Loco informed as the crew started to station themselves on the porch. John frowned. He knew there were two reasons why Loco stated no hangin' out. Either Killa did not want them to hang or the beef with the Bloods was starting to kick back up again. Even though John knew that these would be the reasons that he and his crew couldn't hang out, for his own satisfaction, he decided to pick his brother's brain.

"What's the problem?"

"Killa said not to, alright".

"Why?" John asked.

"Don't worry about it," Loco snarled, "Now, take yo' ass in the house!"

John shrugged his shoulders, looked at Little Loco and whispered," Say something."

Loco treated Little Loco like they were brothers and John like a step-brother. John knew that he would give more information to Loco than he.

Little Loco gave a puzzled look "Why we gotta go? We can't kick it?"

"It aint cool, Little…"

John smacked his lips before Loco could finish his sentence. "It aint cool," meant a war between the Crips and Bloods was about to kick off. This meant no hanging out because things could get rough and dangerous. Loco gave John the evil eye. He thought John had smacked his lips at him. He snapped "Nigga, I told you about smackin' yo' lips like a bitch er' time you don't get yo' way! Take yo' ass in the house before I fuck you up!"

Loco squirted. His whole demeanor changed. John knew what that meant. Loco was the disciplinarian of the family. He was built like a linebacker and had hands as good as Mike Tyson's in the 80's. And when Loco got mad, he was mad! Other than God, Loco was the only man that John feared. John stood hardcore in front of his homies, but knew not to play with Loco. He gave his boys dap and they all parted separate ways.

That night when Mama made it home, she cooked, cleaned, took a shower, and gave John a lecture before falling asleep. That was her normal routine, especially when she worked a long day or had done overtime. His mother worked so hard that Killa told her on many occasions to stop working and move out of the hood. He had all the money needed, but Mama wasn't going for it. She didn't want to move out of the hood with his money and she told him, "Benjamin, I will never! By the color of my Black skin, move some place else

NATURAL BORN KILLAZ

with that "puppet money" you're making. I don't care if you buy me some place that costs you fifty million, I will not leave!"

His mother hated the fact that Killa was a general on the streets and knew he was only being used as a pawn, because he sold what she called, "The White Man's Poison." In Mama's opinion, he was living up to the White man's, statistics and helping them destroy the Black race and culture, by selling crack.

John let out a deep breath when he heard his Mama start to preach. He knew he was about to be in for a long lecture. He got the same lecture every night before she went to sleep. Tonight was no exception; she cornered him in the kitchen.

"John, them White people love to brainwash Black folks and try to make us believe we got to sell that poison. Make us believe that we gotta gangbang, rob, and kill to survive,"

Mama paused for a moment just to make sure everything sunk in. She continued where she left off, "I'm telling you, if that's the case, shit don't stink! They brainwash us for their profit. The prison industry is the highest paid industry in the world. Now ask yourself who own them? I'll tell you who own them, the White man Oppressor. Who fill them? Blacks are who fills them; Blacks and minorities. So with all this knowledge you should know to pay no attention to your brothers. No attention! Because I'm sorry to say, but it's only a matter of time before they're dead or in jail."

Every night John was in for a speech or two. Mama knew he was falling for the streets like his brothers already had. However, most of the knowledge she spoke on about the streets went in one ear and came out the other. John was naive to the fact and was not street wise at all.

That night before John fell asleep; Killa came into his room and sat at the end of his bed. "I heard Momma givin' you her Black Power lecture again!"

TERRY WROTEN

They shared a chuckle, but Killa had a stone look on his face, "Believe me, I hate hearing her tell you the same stuff er'day. I went through it too, so I know how you feel but…"

When the word "but" came out of Killa's mouth, John began to tremble. He knew he was in for another lecture. Mama's words were so powerful they got under Killa's skin, and stayed there nagging at him, even when he was miles away from her.

"John, Mama is tellin 'the truth. I'm a bad example. I got plenty money, more than I need. Millions! But the White man got billions!! Right now, I'm just his field animal. I'm destroying our people with the product he's put in this hood. I'm like the devil's advocate. I'm like a fly trapped in a spider's web."

"Damn," John thought, "Killa is trippin' again!"

Killa was letting Mama's words eat him alive. And John just couldn't understand how? To John, Killa was going crazy!

"John, I'm tellin' you! The White man can come and take me away today, and I won't have nothing! I know I started you claimin' this Blue shit, but it's not the life for a young Black man like you."

Killa glared as if he wanted to cry. John knew Killa was coming from the heart with every word that he spoke, so he gave him his full undivided attention.

"I'm tellin' you this because I love you. I mean, I love you and your whole crew. I know y'all pushin' the hood, because my stupid ass influenced y'all, but gangbangin' is not the life.

Killa was right. He was the one who had John, Kev, and their crew claming Crip. He was the one who had given them blue rags and said, "Go represent." He was the one who encouraged them, and he was the one they looked up to. Sad to say, John and his boys were born into friction. It was their destiny to become a Crip. It was like how some kids became doctors and lawyers, because their father, their older siblings, or whomever they idolized, were doc-

doctors and lawyers, because their father, their older siblings, or whomever they idolized, were doctors or lawyers. As a very small child John knew he was going to become a Gangsta Crip, so he told Killa that he understood by being born in the hood they were all products of their environment.

"You right!" he said. "I can't choose your life for you, but listen to me... Gangbangin' aint shit! John, I don't want you to be like me. I'm a loser!"

Tears rushed to Killa's eyes. He tried to hide them, but they started rolling down his cheeks in rivers. It was getting under his skin that John was on the verge of becoming a full fledged Crip. He was hurting within. Crippin' was something he resented. Everything he loved or cared about was taken away from him due to his dedication to the Crips. He lost many of his conrads either to jail or the streets, and the same fate was now looming over his youngest brother.

"John, you aint even experienced life yet, your only fourteen. This shit I'm doing aint nothing compared to all the beautiful things outside the hood."

"Man, whatever you do, I just want you to promise me that you'll be Mama's first son to graduate from high school, since me and Loco failed to do so. I need you to get a diploma for me and for Mama."

John shook his head an agreement. He couldn't imagine how hard it was going to be for him to graduate from high school. To him, Killa was trippin'. He felt he needed to change the subject. Plus, he needed to ask Killa something that he felt was more of importance.

"Benjamin, can I ask you something?"
"Speak your mind..."

TERRY WROTEN

John stuttered, "How do... How do I get a girl to like me? Should I walk her home?"

John asked that one question and Killa's face lit up. He was surprised that John asked about a girl. He thought his younger brother was too caught up with gangbangin' and girls didn't cross his mind. This surprised Killa so much that when they started talking about Donita, an episode of "New York Undercover" was scheduled to come on TV shortly, and that was Killa's favorite show. By the time their conversation ended that episode of

"New York Undercover" had finished, and his girlfriend Ebony was ready to go home.

Killa and Ebony had an "A" list house in what niggas in the hood called "rich mans land." Anything that was out of the grip of poverty was "rich mans land" to hood niggas; even regular middle class neighborhoods were called 'rich mans land'. Killa and Ebony lived in Malibu. They lived in the real suburbs.

When Ebony came walking into the room, John looked at Killa and chuckled. He knew Killa didn't want to leave, but Ebony had Killa on lock. He turned to John and said, "Look, to sum er'thing up, if you walk Donita home and ask her to go to the movies with you, I'll letchu borrow my Lexus. And if you want, I'll take you shopping afterwards."

Surprisingly, Killa was encouraging John to walk Donita home. It didn't seem to bother him that Donita's brothers were his arch-rivals. John knew Killa's deal sounded too good to be true, especially the bit about driving Killa's car. However, it wasn't long before he showed his true colors.

"You can borrow the car after you and Kevin work for me on Saturday. Loco, Crip Van, and the rest of us gotta go to the Westside, so I'll need y'all to work the spots for me."

NATURAL BORN KILLAZ

Killa was a hypocrite. He was unpredictable. One minute he was anti-White man and saying no to the streets, then the next he was Mr. Crip Himself, and calling all the shots. Killa was fighting his own demons. Most street niggas go through this when they're rattling the fence of retirement. It's similar to how an addict goes through withdrawl when trying to kick an addiction.

"Oh yeah! Another thing! If you walk that girl home, do not cross that borderline. And you know what I'm talkin' about."

John knew exactly what Killa was talking about, so he assured him that he would not cross the borderline of the Crip and the Blood's territories. He sensed that Killa wasn't too infatuated with their overall talk. It seemed to him that Killa was troubled with expressing himself. He knew Killa's night would be long and that he would question those demons. He rolled over in bed and fell asleep.

Wroten Killa Black
Chapter Three
Killa
Friday, February 11th 1994

Killa snapped as he and Ebony lay in bed. He blurted "Damn cuzz!" He was pressed because John was claiming Crips and found it hard to accept. Ebony sensed his frustrations, propped herself up on a pillow and said, "You stressin' over John and his crew again, huh?" Killa nodded. He was lost in thought.

"Benjamin," she said "You act like you can't tell them boys what to do. Everyone on the Eastside knows you are the leader of the whole organization, so if you don't want them to join, stop letting them hang! You make it worse, because all of 'em look up to you. I'm not tryna get on your case, but you are the reason they're doing the things they do. You let them hang and claim like it's the thing to do. Then, you come home and stress about it. I can see with my own two eyes that your conscious is killin' you, and these streets are finally getting the best of you. You let them work the spots; and they make so much money, they loving it."

Killa was tempted to tell her to shut the hell up, but he needed someone to vent to.

"Ebony, I didn't ask to hear everything I already know! You makin' it harder on me while I'm tryna softing the load. Cuzz, you dwellin' on shit I already know."

A look of irritation spread across Ebony's face, "I'm just tryna let you know yo' down falls, so if you can't stand the heat stay the hell outta the kitchen."

"I'm not trippin' 'bout them hustlin'. I'm just kickin' myself in the ass for not puttin' the fire out before it got worse. I let them hang and claim, knowing they really don't have a clue about the street life like they think"

"Benjamin, can you please get to the point? I'm tired and I'm not tryna stay up all night with you."

The time was almost two o'clock, Killa frowned. He needed to express himself and wasn't getting any support.

"The problem is, I got a non-supportive-ass baby momma. If you don't wanna talk, I'll go talk to my son."

Benjamin III, Killa's three-year-old son, was asleep in his room.

"Please don't wake him," said Ebony. "And don't start actin' like a spoiled ass baby ya-damn-self. You know I'm here for you. All I'm askin' is that you don't take all night unless you're hungry."

Killa smiled, Ebony knew how to put a smile on his face.

"Okay," he said "let me get this off my chest because you could feed me any day, and I'm hungry as hell. But first, I'm just worried that things are starting to flare back up with the Bloods, and it will hurt me bad if something happen to John or anyone in his crew. I already lost my best friend to this bullshit, and I'm not tryna lose nobody else. I've told Loco to stop lettin' them hangout, but he told me that even if they're not hangin' they're all still claimin'. He told me John and his crew are already 'out there', and known by a few of the Bloods. I just think Loco wants Nathan to be Little Loco so bad, I can't tell if he's lying to me or what!"

Ebony shook her head and grinned. She knew Killa was in denial. It didn't take a rocket scientist to see that John and his crew were full fledged wannabes.

"Baby, Loco aint lying, he's right! Those boys are 'out there'."

"The other day, Big Head said to me, 'bitch imma Crip'. And before that, I caught John in the alley, the one near Carver, fighting some Bloods!"

"Hold on! You mean to tell me you caught them fighting with the enemy and you didn't tell me?"

"Well yes,"she said "I didn't think nothing of it. John actually talked me into not tellin' you. The boy played me by saying, 'If you tell Killa, you know he gonna be stressing." He was tellin' the truth, but I'm tellin' you now before something bad happen to one of them."

Killa snapped. "What do you mean before something bad happen to them? What you know that I don't?"

"Benjamin," she sighed. "I don't know anything else except what I just told you."

"However, what I do know is you taught me the game; taught me how to be a snake, so you need to teach them before it's too late. Do you remember how it was?"

Killa ignored the question, rolled over, and turned his back to her.

"I said, do you remember?" Ebony asked again.

"How can I forget," he said rolling back over.

They shared a laugh, "Ha!" and started reminiscing.

CHAPTER 3

KILLA

Friday, February 11th, 1994

Killa snapped as he and Ebony lay in bed. He blurted "Damn cuzz!" He was pressed because John was claiming Crips and found it hard to accept. Ebony sensed his frustrations, propped herself up on a pillow and said, "You stressin' over John and his crew again, huh?" Killa nodded. He was lost in thought.

"Benjamin," she said "You act like you can't tell them boys what to do. Everyone on the Eastside knows you are the leader of the whole organization, so if you don't want them to join, stop letting them hang! You make it worse, because all of 'em look up to you. I'm not tryna get on your case, but you are the reason they're doing the things they do. You let them hang and claim like it's the thing to do. Then, you come home and stress about it. I can see with my own two eyes that your conscious is killin' you, and these streetsare finally getting the best of you. You let them work the spots; and they make so much money, they loving it."

Killa was tempted to tell her to shut the hell up, but he needed someone to vent to.

"Ebony, I didn't ask to hear everything I already know! You makin' it harder on me while I'm tryna softing the load. Cuzz, you dwellin' on shit I already know."

A look of irritation spread across Ebony's face, "I'm just tryna let you know yo' down falls, so if you can't stand the heat stay the hell outta the kitchen."

NATURAL BORN KILLAZ

"I'm not trippin' 'bout them hustlin'. I'm just kickin' myself in the ass for not puttin' the fire out before it got worse. I let them hang and claim, knowing they really don't have a clue about the street life like they think"

"Benjamin, can you please get to the point? I'm tired and I'm not tryna stay up all night with you."

The time was almost two o'clock, Killa frowned. He needed to express himself and wasn't getting any support.

"The problem is, I got a nonsupportive-ass baby momma. If you don't wanna talk, I'll go talk to my son."

Benjamin III, Killa's three-year-old son, was asleep in his room.

"Please don't wake him," said Ebony. "And don't start actin' like a spoiled ass baby ya-damn-self. You know I'm here for you. All I'm askin' is that you don't take all night unless you're hungry."

Killa smiled, Ebony knew how to put a smile on his face.

"Okay," he said "let me get this off my chest because you could feed me any day, and I'm hungry as hell. But first, I'm just worried that things are starting to flare back up with the Bloods, and it will hurt me bad if something happen to John or anyone in his crew. I already lost my bestfriend to this bullshit, and I'm not tryna lose nobody else. I've told Loco to stop lettin' them hangout, but he told me that even if they're not hangin' they're all still claimin'. He told me John and his crew are already 'out there', and known by a few of the Bloods. I just think Loco wants Nathan to be Little Loco so bad, I can't tell if he's lying to me or what!"

Ebony shook her head and grinned. She knew Killa was in denial. It didn't take a rocket scientist to see that John and his crew were full fledged wannabes.

"Baby, Loco aint lying, he's right! Those boys are 'out there'."

"The other day, Big Head said to me, 'bitch imma Crip'. And before that, I caught John in the alley, before that the one near Carver,

TERRY WROTEN

fighting some Bloods!"

"Hold on! You mean to tell me you caught them fighting with the enemy and you didn't tell me?"

"Well yes," she said "I didn't think nothing of it. John actually talked me into not tellin' you. The boy played me by saying, 'If you tell Killa, you know he gonna be stressing." He was tellin' the truth, but I'm tellin' you now before something bad happen to one of them."

Killa snapped. "What do you mean before something bad happen to them? What you know that I don't?"

"Benjamin," she sighed. "I don't know anything else except what I just told you."

"However, what I do know is you taught me the game; taught me how to be a snake, so you need to teach them before it's too late. Do you remember how it was?"

Killa ignored the question, rolled over, and turned his back to her.

"I said, do you remember?" Ebony asked again.

"How can I forget," he said rolling back over.

They shared a laugh, "Ha!" and started reminiscing.

~~~~~~

The year was 1986. It was a cold November night and Killa and Ebony were out nickle and diming and working the pavement. They were both new to the hustle and bustle of the street life and they were learning the grim reality of it all.

"Lemme get a dime," the driver in a 1985 Buick yelled as he pulled up to the block. The car had presidential tint, so Killa approached it with caution. This was the 1980's and crack was rolling like dice at a casino. Killa had crackheads lined up on the block like he was the Summer Lunch Program. Walking to the car, Killa decided to throw caution to the wind. There were too many fiends on the

NATURAL BORN KILLAZ

block to move slowly. Time was money, and money was time. As Killa made it to the car with Ebony at his side, his lips ejaculated "damn!" He'd got caught slippin'.

"Yeah muthafucka you know what's going on? I want it all!"

Killa knew it was a stick up. The driver pulled a pistol. Killa couldn't see inside the car, so he didn't know who was pointing the gun. He wanted to run, but Ebony was right next to him and from the look on her face, he could see she was in a state of shock. He normally carried protection, but this night he was not carrying it with him. He figured he might could out smart the armed bandit.

"Look homie, I got two gees. My girl don't have anything. But on Crip, if you rob me, you will not make it off this block. I got homies posted all around here."

Wroten Killa Black

The window of the car rolled down to reveal OG Midnight. Killa's frown turned to a smile. OG Midnight was Killa's mentor. He was as dark as his name suggested, around thirty-five and stood five-eleven. Being a seventies gangbanger, he was one of the only original Crips left. The rest were either dead or in jail, some were smoked-out, others had moved on giving up the life of gangbangin'. He was the last man standing from his era and he believed, "Crips did not die, they multiplied."

"Killa, what up Lil' Homie? You and your girl are slippin'!"

"Damn", Killa thought "Cuzz got me" Killa had s slipped and could have been easily robbed or killed, but he would have never admit to it.

"Come on cuzz! You know I wasn't slippin'."

Midnight shook his head nonchalantly. He knew Killa was going to be in denial. What was of more interest to him, was the girl at Killa's side at that moment.

TERRY WROTEN

"You and your girl were slippin'. Imma bring you a few gats over here for protection, but first I wanna know who she is? And how old is she"?

Ebony took it up on herself to answer him, before Killa could open his mouth,

"My name is Ebony! I'm fifteen! And why do you wanna know?"

Midnight smiled, Ebony surprised him with her quick and snappy response.

"Why I wanna know," he said. "Well I'll tell you why... Shit, I might have to kill you one day. You could be a snake."

Killa's brow started dripping sweat; he knew exactly what Midnight was hinting at. And to Killa, Midnight was doubting his gansta.

"Midnight, I remember everything you taught me about snakes. And this girl ain't one. She's my queen!"

Midnight nodded, "A'ight, I wont question yo' gangsta no more, but make sure you teach her the game, because right now y'all slippin'!"

Silence, Killa's response was delayed. He leaned on the driver's door, looked at Ebony, and passed her their stash. Ebony turned on her heels and walked away.

"Midnight, on Crip, I'm not slippin'."

"If you weren't slippin', how come I could've had y'all heads and y'all money?"

Killa was caught off guard. He started stuttering, "I mean... I mean...I mean, I didn't know it was you. I was just about to give Lefty, Loco, and Crip Van the signal to light this Buick up."

Not too far away Lefty, Loco, and Crip Van, was camouflaged in bushes on each corner of the block. They were posing as security, and like Killa, they were slippin', because they were unaware of Midnight's presence. However, Killa knew he was wrong and had

NATURAL BORN KILLAZ

to tighten up his game.

"They're in the bushes, by those trees, over there, and over there," Killa said pointing to the various positions. "So who's slippin'?"

Midnight scratched his chin. He had not known that Killa's crew was in the trenches, so he was slippin' too. "Seems to me, we both slippin'," he said. "However, I only drove over to this side of town to tell you about the meeting. You're gon be the man of the hour when you promoted to Lieutenant."

Killa smiled at the news, but he wasn't pleased like most most would be. At the time, he was a Sergeant so moving up the ranks was cool, but he wasn't going to be satisfied until he was a General. Later that night after the entire supple of crack was sold, Loco went home late. Killa and Ebony weren't too far behind, and when they came through the door, Mama looked at Killa with fire in her eyes. Loco was only eleven when Mama found discovered Killa recruited him to sell "poison."

"Benjamin, I heard about how you have your brother sellin' that stuff, and if I find out it's true and that you got him helpin' the White man kill our people, imma put you out and call the police!" Mama was mad, but she would have never called the police on any of her children. That was her favorite statemen, to let her children know she was serious. Nine times out of ten Mama often contradicted herself, because she hated how the police kept locking Black folks up. Mama kept talking until Killa got tired of her ranting.

"Mama alright! I already know how the White man tries to use us as pawns or whatever, but right now me and Ebony is bout to go to my room."

Mama sat down. She was through! She didn't have the skin to accept the fact that Killa was getting caught up in the street life. Tears filled her eyes. Losing Killa to the streets was the first major blow to Mama. She cried herself to sleep that night. She was living a Mother's worst nightmare.

In Killa's room, Ebony wondered just what Midnight meant when he said "teach her the game." She knew trust was a value that was lacking in the Crip community, but could never understand why. All she knew was that she loved Killa no matter what. Although only fifteen, she knew he was the person she wanted to spend her life with. She was a pretty girl with brown eyes, coffee colored skin, long hair, and an hourglass figure. She was a dime. She knew that she could pull any brother, but she only had eyes for Killa. His dark complexion, height, frame, walk, talk, and gangsta charisma was everything that she wanted and needed.

As they sat on his bed kissing, she asked Killa could he explain what Midnight meant by "teach her"

Killa smirked, Ebony was thinking about the samething he was. He'd been trying to figure out the best way to go about finding out if she was really his queen.

He asked, "Do you love me?"

Ebony replied, "Yes."

"How much?"

"I love you with all my heart."

"All your heart?"

"All of it," Ebony smiled.

"So my last breath is your last breath?"

"Yes," she said "Your last breath is mines, I promise."

Killa could read the truth in her beautiful brown eyes. He instantly knew she meant everything she was saying. Killa was quiet for awhile, thinking of his next approach,

"Will you ride with me, till death do us part?"

"Whachu think? You don't know I love you? I'll always ride with you. I'll ride till we die. You are my life and I'll do anything to keep

NATURAL BORN KILLAZ

you!" Ebony was sprung. She really loved Killa.

She sighed, "Look Benjamin I'm not stupid. I care about you. All you gotta do is tell me what you want me to do."

Ebony was bold. She knew all along that she had to prove herself. What she didn't know was exactly what she had to do to prove herself, but as long as Killa told her what she had to do, she was all game.

"A'ight, since you think you got what it takes let me tell you the deal."

Killa dealt her the instructions and the game that night. Ebony set out and played her cards. Within two months, she learned how to seduce, manipulate, strategize, and dehumanize. Ebony became Killa's certified queen in a short time. During the months that followed, she helped lure a general in the Bloods organization to his death. Ebony led the general from the Bloods to believe that she was twenty-two year old college girl. Impressed, the general fell for her and when it was arranged to meet this one of a kind sista, he drove right into trouble. This gave her stripes.

She waited for him on a dead end street close to the college. But when he pulled up to the curb, she walked away. Her signal was the tap of her heel, signaling "that's him," that gave Killa, Crip Van, Loco, and Lefty the go ahead. They came seemingly from out of nowhere, spraying bullets. The General was trapped. He had no place safe to go. He tried to put his Cutlass in reverse, but bullets penetrated the car and the General. The scene was not pretty.

~~~~~~

Ebony's reminiscing about the past was her way of making her point. Killa knew exactly where she was going with the conversation, so he let her finish.

"Baby all I'm saying is, them boys wanna be out there so they need to be laced with the game before it's too late. Before one of 'em get crossed up. I know you don't want them gangbangin', but people already think they're Crips. You should at least school them. You gotta let them know all the down falls of gangbangin', tell them the dangers, tell them how Lefty died."

Killa sighed and shook his head. As much as he didn't want to admit it, Ebony was talking the truth.

"Damn, you're right! But there's another problem."

Ebony was getting irritated, she was sleepy. Her eyes were burning and now Killa wanted to talk about another problem. She groaned, "Now what?"

Killa took a deep breath, "John has a crush on Brazy B's sister. I've encouraged him to walk her to the borderline because he really likes her, but I'm worried. Trust is a value that I don't have. I don't know what I'll do if one of them dudes try to get at him because of me."

Ebony was exhausted, but she knew she had to show affection to her man. She kissed him on the lips and said, "Baby, you can't keep stressin' over John and his crew. All you can do is guide them and hope they'll learn from your mistakes. John is smarter than what you think, so stop worryin'. Walkin' that little girl to the borderline might start something positive, so please, just stop thinkin' negative all the time.

CHAPTER 4

The next day after John's long brotherly talk with Killa, he sat in Miss Phillips's class contemplating his next move. He sat trying to catch eye contact with Donita, but she never looked his way. Not only did she ignore him, she also turned her chair so she didn't have to see him. "Little slob bitch," he mumbled to himself heated. lla snapped as he and Ebony lay in bed. He blurted "Damn cuzz!" He was pressed because John was claiming Crips and found it hard to accept. Ebony sensed his frustrations, propped herself up on a pillow and said, "You stressin' over John and his crew again, huh?" Killa nodded. He was lost in thought.

"Benjamin," she said "You act like you can't tell them boys what to do. Everyone on the Eastside knows you are the leader of the whole organization, so if you don't want them to join, stop letting them hang! You make it worse, because all of 'em look up to you. I'm not tryna get on your case, but you are the reason they're doing the things they do. You let them hang and claim like it's the thing to do. Then, you come home and stress about it. I can see with my own two eyes that your conscious is killin' you, and these streetsare finally getting the best of you. You let them work the spots; and they make so much money, they loving it."

Killa was tempted to tell her to shut the hell up, but he needed someone to vent to.

NATURAL BORN KILLAZ

John just knew Donita was on the Red and Blue trip, so he started scribbling "CRIP" on his desk as he thought of another approach to get at her. He was under extreme pressure. He had to get Donita to be his girlfriend or he was going to get disciplined. A discipline meant nothing if you knew how to fight, but John didn't feel like getting jumped by his friends. Plus, he wanted Donita to be his future wife. He was so deep in thought, Miss Phillips caught him scribbling on the desk.

"John, what are you doing? Didn't we already talk about this nonsense," she said glaring at the desk. "Didn't I tell you and your homeboys to stop writing that Crip stuff all over school?!"

Miss Phillips was heated. She had told John over a thousand times to stop writing Crip everywhere; especially in her class and in her books. He'd promised one too many times not to write on her stuff, so she snapped. "Boy this is my last time telling you and them other boys about destroying this school!"

It was easy to tell when Miss Phillips was heated because she went from calling John and his boys "young Black men" to 'Wannabes'. After his talk with her, she had the right to call him a wannabe. Miss Philliphs was hood but classy, professional and intelligent, and John respected her gangsta.

"Now get that Ajax and scrub pad, before I get real mad!"

John chuckled as he got up to clean the graffiti from the desk, because Donita smiled and gave him a look that read, "you're crazy."

John smiled back and nodded, 'Wassup". He couldn't believe she acknowledged him, so after cleaning up the mess he made, he sat back in at his desk and did as Killa informed him during there brotherly talk. He wrote her a letter.

Dear Donita,

What it do? This is John. I really like you and want to know can I take

TERRY WROTEN

you to the movies this weekend.

The letter was brief but to the point. When the bell for nutrition rang, John leapt up from his desk and gave her the letter.

"After you read it, let me know your answer at lunch," he said smiling like the Kool Aide man.

~~~~~~

During nutrition, John met with his friends at the gym. It was a Friday, so Mr. Rudy had Big Boi on the turntables and the gym was crackin' like a house in the 80's. Kev secured a spot in front of the line for John and asked, "What it is?" as John made it over.

Knowing what Kev was referring to, John smirked and shook his head at the same time. John had told Kev his plans earlier that morning, "Cuzz! Like I said it is what it is. I'm still tryna make Miss Jackson my girl."

Little Loco blurted, "Awwww, cuzz! You shot her a letter?"

"Fool, whatchu think? You know I did! We'll find out what's her answer at lunch."

John could tell just by looking at Mike that he was feeling threatened. Mike started questioning his gangsta. Mike wanted to be the only player in the crew. He already had a few fine girls from off the Westside, but he knew if John pulled Donita that John was going to be "The Man" and not him.

Mike looked John dead in the eyes and spatted, "Cuzz, is that right? You think she wanna fuck with yo' black ass, or a playa like me?"

The crew paid their way into the gym, which was only fifty cents. They took their seats at the bleachers; it was common knowledge at Carver the bleachers were theirs. As they sat down, John turned to Mike and said, "Yeah that's right! Ima have the finest girl in school. Matter of fact, give me till Monday if not today."

NATURAL BORN KILLAZ

John's bragging got to Kev and he cut him off, "Yeah cuzz, whatever. If you get Donita, I'll get somebody else. I'm not gonna doubt your gangsta, so I got somebody else in mind."

Big Head was just about to add his two cents, but "Daisy Duke" by the 69 Boys started playing and the whole gym went crazy. The dancers hit the floor like they were at a Luke party. Daisy Duke was a party anthem, so it got the party started.

John had his eyes locked on Donita and her best friend Me-Me, who he knew Kev was going to get at. Me-Me was the second prettiest in school, she stood around five foot six, weighed around a hundred and twenty pounds, her skin resembled dark chocolate, and her hair was long and silky. She was fourteen and ghettoified to say the least. She came from the Projects, so around school her nickname was "Miss Ghetto." No other female on the planet was more ghetto than her. She went by the name Me-Me, but her birth name was Meosha.

As Me-Me and Donita ran to the middle of the gym to dance, John and the crew stayed posted. They were Crip Wannabes, they didn't have time for fun and games. They stood in the bleachers watching everything and acting hard.

Meosha dropped her math book as she ran to the dance floor. She was so loud-mouthed and excied, she didn't realize she dropped it. John wasn't surprised that Kev had seen her drop it and he flew down the bleachers to pick it up. Money Mike was thinking the same thing as John.

He yelled, "Kev, don't help that bitch, you know she don't like us."

"Yeah cuzz," Big Head added. "Let that bitch get her own shit!"

Little Loco had to let his presence be known, "Nigga, fuck that bitch! Let her shit stay where it's at."

TERRY WROTEN

The whole crew knew that Mike was right, but no one said a word. Meosha's family were the Project Bloods, they were arch rivals. They knew she didn't like them, but Kev didn't care. It didn't come as a shock Kev was testing his macking game, that was his character. Meosha was the second finest girl in school, since Don was courting Donita, Kev was determined to pull her. Being best friends John and Kev competed with everything; this was their way of growing up.

John watched as he walked over and tried to hand her the book. When Meosha's head started moving from side to side, he knew she was saying something smart. Kev immediately turned on his heels and walked off. Meosha followed, she was saying something but the words were hard to make out because the music was too loud.

When they made it to the bleachers, John overheard the end of their conversation,

"Kevin, you betta give me my muthafuckan book! I'm not playin' witcha ol' midget ass!"

"Cuzz, you think I care?" Kev snarled. "I was tryna' be nice to yo' muhfuckan ass. But, since you tryna get all stupid with a nigga, cuzz, I'll give you yo' book when I want too. This a Crip thing over here."

After nutrition, John went to third and fourth period; they were the longest two periods he'd ever sat through. He was so anxious to meet up with Donita, he looked at the clock every other minute, waiting for 11:30. When 11:30 arrived, John met his boys at the lunch tables. As they posted at the tables Big Head blurted, "Awww, cuzz! Here come Donita and Miss Ghetto."

John turned and smiled. Donita had his letter in her hand and was approaching the crowd.

She walked up and said, "Okay, I'll go."

NATURAL BORN KILLAZ

"We'll meet after school," John replied. "I'll walk you home, so we could talk about when, where, and what movie you wanna see?"

"That won't be a good idea," she said.

John shook his head. He knew exactly what she was talking about. John was claiming Crip, and his whole family was Crips, and they wore nothing blue. Her family was Bloods and wore red. Her family and John's family were enemies, but John wasn't worried about the families' disputes. He just wanted Donita to be his girlfriend. Nonetheless, he had to prove a point to his boys. Everyone in his crew had experienced sex, except him. He wanted to show them that he got pussy and he was going to be fucking the finest girl in school.

"Why wouldn't that be a good idea? Cause of yo' brothers?"

"Yep!" She answered. "My brothers and their homeboys will kill you."

John snapped, he didn't take easy to people threatening him.

"I don't care, I'm not afraid of yo' brothers. I just wanna walk you home."

John insisted that he walk her home, he insisted so much he'd forgot that Killa told him not to walk her pass the borderline.

Donita agreed, "You can walk me home at your own risk."

"That's a deal," John replied smiling like the cat that swallowed the canary.

~~~~~~

After school, John met up with Donita at Jack-In-The-Crack. The whole crew had walked to the restaurant with him, all except Kev. He'd waited in front of Kev's class after last period, but Kev never came out. He knew then that Kev had pulled a slick one to walk Me-Me home.

When Donita entered the restaurant, John smiled. He gave his boys a look that read:

TERRY WROTEN

Yeah, I did that.

Donita returned the smile. John just knew he was The Man.

"What it do sexy?" he asked. "Are you hungry?"

John used Killa's advice and offered to treat. He stayed with a pocket full of money, so treating Donita to a meal wasn't a problem. However, she was bashful she said, "That's okay." John knew why she was acting bashful. He looked his crew and said, "Cuzz, y'all corn breading."

The crew chuckled in unison and blurted, "Awww, cuzz!" They got the code and walked off. Corn breading was code for cockblocking.

Before walking off Mike said, "A'ight, cuzz, I'll see you tomorrow at the spot."

The crew parted ways and exchanged daps.

After John's team disappeared in the wind, he looked at Donita and sensed she didn't like being around Crips.

"What?" he asked, letting her know he sensed her animosity.

Donita twisted her lips, "Do y'all really wanna be Crips?"

"Yep, why you ask that?"

Donita raised her eyebrows. "Because that boy y'all call Big Head…"

"Who Wesley?"

"Yeah that's him."

"What about him?"

"Well, he shouldn't be claiming Crip, because he let Bool Aid punk him in front of my house the other day."

John laughed, "Is that right?"

"And he wasn't claiming Crips then," she said shaking her head matter factly.

John nodded and shook his head smiling. Donita was getting on his boy Head, and he wasn't going for it.

NATURAL BORN KILLAZ

"Come on, get off my boy, he aint no Super Crip. Plus, I already put hands on Bool Aide. He was lucky my brother's baby momma came outta nowhere, because I was gonna smash him."

Donita could see that John didn't like her talking about his boys, so she decided to the change the subject, "Can we move on to the next subject, Mr. Super Wannabe?"

Calling John a Wannabe struck his heart like a Mack truck into a wall. John was a Wannabe, but in his heart he wasn't.

"Yeah whatever," he said. "But I'm not a wannabe. Imma Crip! Anyway are you hungry or what?"

"No, but you can buy me something to drink."

"Like what?"

"Like a strawberry milkshake, large."

As John walked over to the counter to order two large milkshakes, he told himself, "Damn, this girl is picky."

After placing the order and handing Donita her drink he asked, "Are you ready to go?"

She looked at John with her pretty cat eyes and replied, "Are you serious? Because if so, we both 'bout to be in some shit."

Mama had always taught John that the only thing to fear is fear itself. He said, "Baby, I'm as serious as a fat bitch having an asthma attack."

That punch-line worked 'cause Donita agreed, "Let's Go."

As they walked to Donita's house, John thought about all the advice Killa had given him. However, he was ignoring the advice about crossing the borderline. He thought long and hard about turning around when they reached the dividing line of both sects, but found himself into more trouble by remembering his other advice.

"Oh Yeah! I think I'm suppose to be carryin' yo' books."

She nodded, "I thought you woulda been asked."

"I only just thought about it. I actually didn't know I had to carry yo' books. Imma Crip! We don't carry books," he lied. He was trying to play the hardcore role. "Naw, I'm just playin'."

Being a young gentleman he grabbed her books, "My brother told me to carry yo' book last night when we were talking about you and a few other things."

Donita looked at John as if she didn't believe him, "So you and yo' brother been plannin' this all along."

"Yep. I tell my brother er'thing. And to keep it gangsta witchu, er'body in my family knows I have a crush on a girl named Donita Jackson."

"Yeah right."

"That's on er'thing."

"Well, I like you too."

John's eyes lit up, this was music to his ears. He went for the kill, "So does that make you my girl?"

She snap-finger-fast countered, "I don't know because every girl in school likes you."

John was popular with the females at school. They all tried to give him play, but he never took the bait. Killa always taught him to watch out for snakes, so he looked at all females as snakes until they proved themselves otherwise. This was a bad way to look at women, but John was a young upcoming hoodstar, so he had to be cautious with everyone.

John countered balancing out the charts, "And every boy in school have a crush on you. Only yesterday my best friend and Mike had a fight over you."

"Stop lyin'! I don't even know Michael like that. And Kevin 'the midget' likes Meosha."

John laughed, "Ha! No he don't! Nobody likes "Miss Ghetto"."

NATURAL BORN KILLAZ

That was a lie. Me-Me didn't like Crips, so John decided to take up for Kev, just in case he was turned down. It was at that moment he realized that Kev was most likely walking Meosha home. He stopped in the mid-stride of their walk and blurted, "damn!" to himself. He was hoping Kev didn't walk Me-Me into the Projects with all that blue he had on. However, John was blued down from head to toe too, he even had two blue rags hanging out of his back left pocket, everything about his outfit screamed C-R-I-P. He couldn't worry too much about Kev, thinking over all the blue he was draped in himself. Entering enemy territory he thought, "Cuzz, whatta fuck I'm doin'?" but he continued to walk.

John tried to get Donita to agree to bei his girl, but he only succeeded at getting her phone number, a hug, and a promise to go to the movies.

"Damn cuzz, why I cross that borderline," was all he could say as they arrived at her house. He looked at her brothers and their homeboys mean-mugging him, and his heart began to skip a beat. He didn't know what got into him, but he knew that he had made a stupid move by going against his brother's advice. He knew there was no turning back. He thought 'if I die today, it's over chasing some pussy. Imma sucka because that's not the way to go out. Especially not for a Gangsta Crip."

John walked himself into a death trap and it was time to face the consequence for the choices he made. He recognized three of the enemies off top, and instantly knew there were going to be problems. They all held hatred for himself, family, and his side of the city. He spotted Bool Aid immediately, they'd had a fighting war and it was on sight between them. They fought on three different occasions, and John smashed Bool Aide each time. Bool Aide was one of those niggas who didn't know how to fight, but stayed trying. Donita's brothers Brazy and Bay-Bay, were John's brothers' worst enemies. The two pairs were like the Hatfield's and McCoy's.

"Who is that?" Brazy B asked Donita. He was the first to make his presence known. "That betta' not be Killa and Loco's little brother."

John was caught slippin' and the Bloods were approaching from all angles. He had no choice but to stand his ground, "Yeah, it's me!" John was no punk, but he wasn't stupid either. Brazy B was a known killer. John told himself, "If I see any movement towards a burner, I'm jumpin' behind Donita". John knew they wouldn't do anything to hurt her, so Donita was going to be his shield because he was trapped.

Stunned from John's boldness Brazy B shook his head, "Whachu doing on this side of town?"

John hesitated before answering. Brazy B stood about five foot eleven, so John wasn't worried about throwing punches with him. He was more worried about him pulling a gun. He was a general within the Bloods' community and a known professional killer on the streets. He was considered royalty on the Bloods side of town and known to have a cold trigger finger. Brazy B was young, around twenty-two with a vicious track record. Whatever he said went!

John thought hard before answering the question, "I'm just walking your sister home..."

He paused to catch himself from saying the word "cuzz". That could have been a fatal mistake. He didn't need to give Brazy B any more reasons to kill him.

"I'm just walking your sister home and making sure she's safe."

Brazy chuckled, he liked John's response. It was smooth. He could tell John liked his younger sister. The boy had taken a life threatening chance to cross the borderline and walk his home.

"You like my sister, huh?"

NATURAL BORN KILLAZ

John smiled. He could sense the Bloods weren't trippin' and Brazy B decided not to kill him. Donita had stayed right at his side; it was as if she was going to fight with him against her brothers.

"Yeah I like your sister," he answered. "If I didn't, I wouldn't be over here. I knew she was y'all sister before I asked to walk her home, so I'm not trippin', I'm just walking her home."

John was street smart and quick on the draw. Brazy smiled and nodded. He looked as if he was in a state of shock the whole time John stood there. This was a love/hate relationship. As much as Brazy B hated John's brothers, there was a time when things were different. Mama raised him, and there was a time that Brazy and Killa were friends, but the Red and Blue changed everything.

Brazy B pointed at John, "First off, me and your brothers got issues. They don't like me, and I sure as hell don't like them. That mean I'm suppose to be settin' an example, but since I still got love for yo' Momma, Imma give you a pass. I can tell Donita likes you, so as long as you keep her safe and happy, we won't have any problems. You dig?"

John immediately shook his head in agreement to his pass.

"And when you come over to this side leave all that blue at home, a'ight?"

Bool Aid snapped. According to him, John wasn't supposed to get a pass. He was anticipating murder. He wanted John's head and was hotter than the Mojave Desert on a hot summer day, that Brazy wasn't thinking the same thing as him.

"Fuck! Blood, you gon let blood get away that easy?"

"Nigga, who run this shit, Blood?" Brazy spat.

Bool Aid answered defeated, "You!"

"Okay, shut the fuck up then!" Brazy yelled.

Bool Aid may have been defeated, but he wasn't going to let John walk in and out of his hood without making it hard. He knew that

TERRY WROTEN

John would never give him a pass, so he wasn't going to give him one.

"Well, lemme get a head up with blood."

John laughed to himself. Bool Aide wanted his head so bad, he let his mouth over lead his ass. John knew he was about to knock Bool Aide out. He couldn't go toe to toe with John if his life depended on it.

Brazy started laughing. He liked seeing young soldiers fight. He wasn't trippin' over Bool Aid and John squabbling, squabbling was an art of war and a way of life. It came with the territory of gang-bangin'.

Brazy agreed on the challenge, commanding Bool Aid not to lose. John knew once approved it was time for battle. He balled his fist and slammed it into his palm. He planned to knock Bool Aid out with the first punch. He looked over towards Donita and then to all the bloods that were surrounding him. He knew the g-code, hee knew he was about to get jumped. He knew that if he was Bool Aid and the Bloods were Crips, it wouldn't have been a fair fight. That was something people did on the streets; jumped in and looked after each other, especially if your boy or comrade was being beat.

Donita was thinking the same as John. She knew the situation he was in wasn't fair. She grabbed his hand and said "No John, just go home. You know, if you win what they gonna do. You don't gotta fight!"

Brazy cut her off, "Donita move!"

The Bloods moved out into the street. Bool Aid was walking in a circle. He had taken his shirt off and was slapping his fist into his palm. John stood on the sidewalk, right in front of Donita's house. She repeatedly told him to leave. He was debating should he walk away, stand his ground, or run? He knew the safe route to go, but his pride wouldn't let him go out the cowardly way. His thoughts

NATURAL BORN KILLAZ

were cut off by Brazy yelling, "Move" to Donita again.

"Girl, we aint gon hurt yo' boyfriend. And just because I still have love for Miss Wilson, he can get a fair one. So move!"

That was sweet music to John's ears. He sighed and shook his head. He was getting the chance to smash Bool Aid in front of his homeboys without them jumping in. Donita was still scared for his well-being and at that very moment, John knew for sure that she had feelings for him.

He cracked a one-sided smile and said, "Don't trip! I got hands like Muhammad Ali."

Donita was use to her brothers smashing Crips and sending them along their way on stretchers or to the morgue, so she wasn't buying anything that Brazy said. She was stubborn and the last thing she wanted was for John to get hurt because he walked her home. She waved him off, "John that don't mean anything, these niggaz are scandelous. They still might jump you."

"Look Donita," John said pointing to Bool Aid, "This busta can't see me, and to show you how positive I am, I'll make you a deal. If I win then you gotta be my girl. If I don't, I'll walk right outta here and you don't even have to talk to me again, that is, if you don't want to."

John was willing to fight for what he wanted. He knew this victory would be easy.

The two young soldiers squared off in the middle of the street. John could sense Bool Aide was having second thoughts, and didn't really want to fight. He looked him in the face and laughed. Bool Aide was a light-bright nigga that looked White, and the redness in his cheeks told John that this kid was shitting bricks. John was about to punish him. Bool Aide stood around five foot ten, weighing in at about a hundred and seventy five pounds. John had the reach and weight over him, so he faked a right hook to get the fight on its way. Bool Aide jumped back to avoid the punch, but John followed the fake right hook with a quick left one. Bool Aide didn't know what hit him when that left hook collided with his jaw like a freight train into a wall. He hit the ground head first. John jumped back on his heels waiting for the ram-pack from Bool Aide's crowd, but it never happened.

Brazy stayed true to his word. He yelled, "Go get this fool some water!"

Bool Aid was laid out. John was still worried about how the other Bloods would react, but they weren't trippin' and he couldn't tell if it was from Brazy's command or the way Bool Aid had been laid out. It got comical when he woke up from being knocked out and asked, "What happened?"

Brazy laughed, "Nigga, you got knocked the fuck out."

It was off the hook that Friday, and things were moving fast. Like in the movie "Friday" Ice Cube stated, "It was just another Friday in the hood." This was a life of a young Wannabe in South Central. Shit happened nonstop.

Stunned from the outcome, Donita came running to give John a hug. He knew she feared for him, but he'd made her day when Bool Aid hit the ground. Bool Aide was one of her brother's homeboys whom she couldn't stand. She was glad John put him to shame in front of the other Bloods.

Donita was so happy she asked, "Wanna meet my mom?"

"Hell naw. I already been through enough for one day. Girl, a nigga don't wanna meet yo' mama right now," John thought.

John was lost for words, "Naw that's... naw that's okay. I gotta go meet Kev somewhere," he lied.

At that very moment, Kev was the only person that came to mind.

NATURAL BORN KILLAZ

As John lied, Bay Bay was ear hustling,"Don't be afraid now nigga, Momma don't bite."

John grinned. Bay Bay was one of those nosey dudes whom always had his nose in somebody's business. He was a cool Lieutenant in the Bloods organization. John estimated that he was five foot five and around two hundred and twenty pounds, he was chubby and looked like the fat boy from the movie "Lean on Me". Bay Bay's dark complexion made him stand out compared to the other members of Donita's family, who were all light skinned. Bay Bay had to carry his belly to walk and he stuttered when he talked. But despite his ugly flaws, he was notorious. It was no doubt, Bay Bay was a killer.

John decided to meet Donita's mother. Miss Jackson was a pretty woman, and by looking at her face you could tell that she was around her early forties. Donita and her mother looked exactly alike. The only difference between the two was that Miss Jackson stood a little taller than her daughter, and she had a very light complexion, resembling an older version of the singer Alicia Keys. Miss Jackson and Donita shared the same hazel cat eyes.

Donita inherited everything from her mother. Everything! Her walk! Her talk! Her smile! Those eyes! Her jet black hair! Her lips! They even had the same characteristics.

As John and Donita walked into the house, Miss Jackson asked, "Donita, who is this boy you bringin' into my house?"

"John Wilson," Donita answered.

"Ma, that's...that's Donita's lil' boyfriend," Bay Bay blurted. He cut Donita off so fast; he barely got out what he was trying to say.

"Boyfriend!" Miss Jackson roared, "Donita can't even spell boyfriend, so how in the hell can she have one?!"

Donita was smart. She spelled boyfriend while rolling her neck. Seeing Donita and her Momma together you could tell that they had a special mother-daughter bond. Miss Jackson smiled after Donita spelled boyfriend and turned her attention to John,

"How old are you?"
"Where do you live?"
"Who are ya parents?"
"How do you know Donita?"
"What kind of grades you get?"
"Are you a gang-member?"
"And why are you wearing all that blue?"

Miss Jackson asked question after question until Brazy interrupted,

"Damn Momma! The boy a'ight. That's Miss Wilson's youngest son. I know you remember Bernard and Benjamin. He's their lil' brother, so stop actin' like the police."

Miss Jackson immediately knew who John was, and as she shook her head He read exactly what she was thinking. She knew how gangs ruined their families and their friendships. With all the blue John had on, she knew he was a Wannabe Crip. However, Miss Jackson didn't trip. She looked at John and accepted him with open arms.

Miss Jackson was a cool, hip, and down to earth mom. The time slipped away and before John knew it, he'd sat for an hour and a half talking with Donita and her family. During that time Miss Jackson made it more than clear that John was to treat her daughter with nothing but respect.

John hung with the Jackson's until it was time for him to go. He played with his timing more than once and knew when he got back to the neighborhood; Killa was going to be pissed to say the least. Donita lived ten blocks away; she lived on 33rd Street and McKinley while he lived on 43rd Place and McKinley. He had to get home and when he told Donita, she smacked her lips,

NATURAL BORN KILLAZ

"Well, can you at least call me when you get home?"

John had feelings stirring inside him that he'd never felt before. He had Donita where he wanted her, and couldn't wait to flaunt her in front of his boys.

He figured, right there and then, it was time to make his move. He countered, "Only if I can hold your hand and tell everybody you're my girl".

She sighed, "You are my boyfriend right?"

John smiled, "All the time."

~~~~~~

When John made it home, the sun was setting and Killa was sitting on the hood of his Bentley, cradling a cup of Coke and Rum. He was deep in thought, he was aware John had crossed the borderline. He was pleased to see his brother and greeted him with a brotherly hug, but there was more than one thing on his mind. His comrade and Lieutenant Dice had been found guilty on his third strike. The charge was possession of sales, and he was sentenced to 25 years to life. However, John was the most important issue at hand.

Killa threw a jab, hitting John directly in the chest. The impact buckled John. "Cuzz, you had me worried. Whatta hell happened?"

"You tread over that borderline, didn't you?"

"Whatta hell's goin' on with you?!"

"Why you coming home so late?"

Silence.

Killa was buzzing. He asked question after question while chastising John. John knew the best solution to the situation was to remain silent. He ignored Killa, but his older brother was on his case like a drill seargant.

"Nigga, you walked her home, after I told you not too! You think I'm stupid? I've been drivin' up and down King since foe o'clock!

TERRY WROTEN

It's now, six-fucking-thirty! Cuzz, you just don't know how much I wanna hurt you right now!"

MLK Junior Boulevard was the street that divided the Red from the Blue. It was a street that held a candle light visual every other night. John knew he had some explaining to do. "Yeah, I had crossed over, even had a squabble with that nigga they call Bool Aide."

John was lucky this night, because Loco was gone in traffic, otherwise he would have gotten a beat down. Killa's face looked like thunder.

John had never seen him so mad. He said, "Come on Killa. Don't trip! I had er'thing under control. I handled my business."

"Whachu mean you handled yo' business?" Killa turned his bottle of rum upside down. "Hold on, let me pour a lil' of this drink out for Lefty."

The liquor started gushing onto the ground. John had never met Lefty, but he was Killa's best friend. He was killed by the Bloods when John was young. It was a retaliation killing, a pay back after a Blood General was gunned down. There was also a rumor that the police had killed Lefty and blamed it on the Bloods. No one knew the full story of Lefty's death, but Lefty was a major loss for Killa. Every time he talked about his best friend, tears filled his eyes. Lefty was like his shadow and every time Killa got drunk he poured out some liquor for Lefty and the other homies that had fallen victim to the streets.

Killa poured the drink out in memory of Lefty, while John explained how he knocked out Bool Aid, given a pass from Brazy B and Bay Bay, and how Miss Jackson questioned him like the Feds. Killa was so surprised that Brazy didn't kill his brother and continued to ask, "What did Brazy do when you knocked Bool Aid out?"

NATURAL BORN KILLAZ

As John was trying to get it into Killa's head that he really did knock Bool Aid out and survived an attack from the Bloods, his cell phone and pager went off at the same time.

"What it do...What...Where he at?"

Sweat started to form on Killa's brow. John sensed from his brother's glare that something was wrong. Killa's eyes looked steel cold and his veins started pulsating through his purple skin.

"What's wrong?" John asked.

Killa stared at him in silence then said, "Come on."

They climbed into his Bentley and headed toward the Projects. John instantly started thinking about Kev and at that very moment Killa said, "Kev got shot."

John looked at Killa in disbelief until he saw tears in his eyes. John's heart immediately dropped and images of Kev immediately started to flash through his head.

"Shit! Is he lying in a pool of blood with a white sheet over him?" John thought. His hands started to tremble as he asked, "Where at?"

Tear rushed to his eyes and down his cheek, "God please don't let my best friend be dead."

John was 100% sure that Kev walked Me-Me home, "Damn!" he blurted to himself. "Why he do that?"

"Why?!"

"Why?!!"

"Why?!!!"

No matter how many times John asked himself "why" he couldn't change the answer. The answer was the same reason he walked Donita home, Kev was courting Me-Me to be his girlfriend.

"I don't know where he got shot," Killa informed him, "but Loco and Crip Van just called and said he's at Miss Nina's shop, and to meet up there."

TERRY WROTEN

Miss Nina was a lady in her mid sixties. She knew everyone in the city and hated seeing Black on Black crimes. Miss Nina was part of the Watts Riots and was a community activist. She had every Black person's phone number in South Central. The thrift shop she owned was considered a hood monument. She sold everything that black folks used.

When Killa and John arrived at the shop Loco, Crip Van, and a few other Crips were out front. The shop was on Compton Avenue, which was the borderline between the Project Bloods and the Crips. As they pulled up in the car, John knew guns were within hands reach.

"Where he at?" Killa asked as he and John leapt from his Bentley.

Crip Van pointed towards Miss Nina's shop, "Cuzz bad ass in there."

There were no red or blue lights flashing, so upon arrival one knew that Kev's injuries were not life threatening. John was relieved seeing this.

"The bullet didn't penetrate," Crip Van informed. "It just grazed a piece of skin and meat off his right leg. Miss Nina is playing doctor, so he should be ready in a minute or two. The lil' nigga was walkin' OG Red Flag's niece home, when Little Scottie and two slobs pulled up. The little girl told Kev to run while she tried to stay in the way so Scottie and his boys wouldn't shoot. Kev said when he made it to the corner; Scottie and his boys started bustin', and that's when he fell to the ground from the impact. He said he could hear the little girl Meosha screaming for him to get up or that they were going to kill him. He told me he got up and started runnin' and as he turned the corner; Miss Nina pulled him into her shop and locked the door. Then those bitch-ass-niggas had the nerve to drive by in Scottie's Lexus going two miles an hour lookin' for him!"

"Cuzz, them bitch niggaz tried to kill my brother."

NATURAL BORN KILLAZ

"Okay boys," Miss Nina interrupted while standing at the entrance of her shop, "I'm finish."

Miss Nina was very religious. She knew there was going to be retaliation over Kev's shooting. She said, "Y all come in here and lets pray about it."

It wasn't a mystery that in Los Angeles, the Crips and the Bloods were rivals. Miss Nina thought the best solution to the problem was to pray. John, Kev, and the other Crips gathered in the middle of the shop and Miss Nina ordered the group of young thugs to gather hands. John looked at Kev as they stood in the prayer circle, shook his head, and smiled. He shook his head as if to say, "nigga wait till I tell you!"

Killa, Loco, Crip Van and all the Crips prayed with pistols and crack in their pockets. This was a crazy scenario, but God says, "Come as you are". After reciting the Lords' Prayer Miss Nina said, "And yall remember the Lord says, 'Thou shall not commit adultery, or murder. Thou shall not steal, nor forget to love thy neighbor.'"

Little did Miss Nina know, the Lord couldn't stop what was going to happen next. The God of Gangstas told the Crips something totally different from the God she worshipped, RETALIATION WAS A MUST! It was murder, murder, kill, kill.

CHAPTER 5

CRIP VAN-LOCO

Saturday, February 12th, 1994

Crip Van and Loco had their reputations to uphold. They were Lieutenant-Generals in the hood and weren't taking any loses. They sat uneasy with butterflies in their stomachs caused by the murderous feelings they both felt, and the longer they thought about the stunt Scottie and his cadets had pulled, the more their trigger fingers itched.

As they sat in Crip Van's BMW taking pulls off a blunt he exploded, "Cuzz, fuck them busta-ass- niggas. How the fuck they try to play duck hunt with my lil' brother ,Crip?"

Loco was quiet. He just shook his head and took more pulls of the blunt as Crip Van raved on and on. Them bitch-ass-niggas must don't know who I am?!"

Bang! Crip Van punched the dashboard in frustration.

"But tomorrow they gon' find out who I be! I swear, on Crip! It aint gon' be a pretty sight."

Crip Van was high as a kite, but his face was like thunder and Loco knew he was dead serious. They sat in the BMW talking through the night. Loco was so high all he could do was agree, "Uh huh."

"Yep."

"On Crip."

"Tomorrow."

NATURAL BORN KILLAZ

When the sun came up the following morning both Crips were asleep in the car, where John and his crew found them. Luckily the car was parked in the garage, because they were slippin' and not in the right state of mind. John kicked his foot hard on the garage door and yelled, "Open dis muthafuckan doe,cuzz!"

When Loco emerged from his coma, the door opened and he came out rubbing his eyes. "Cuzz whatta fuck wrong witchu?" he yelled as he ran his hand over the dents that John made in the garage door. By the look on his face, John knew that his brother was about to flip, however. Big Head came to his rescue.

"Damn homie! You and Crip Van were slippin'. Y'all slept in the garage!"

Loco was lost for words. He knew he wasn't practicing what he had preached. He was the one who had been teaching the young Wannabes how to watch their backs. He was also the enforcer who informed the younger crowd to never slip, but here he was doing the exact opposite.

Loco knew Big Head was right, but he tried to redeem himself by saying, "Naw, we never slip, just Crip."

That was a lie. You could smell the chronic on his shirt. John cracked a one-sided smiled at Kev. Kev knowingly smiled back. Kev looked at Loco and said, "Nah, cuzz y'all was slippin; now y'all gotta get disciplined."

The word "discipline" bought Crip Van into sight. He emerged from the garage wiping sleep from his eyes, "Did cuzz just say somethin' about a discipline?"

John laughed and that set off Mike laughing too, because the whole crew knew Kev's favorite word was discipline when somebody did something wrong.

Mike looked at Crip Van and said, "Discipline, that aint nothin' new."

TERRY WROTEN

Lil' Loco stayed quiet because Loco was his big homie but Mike didn't care. "Like Kev just said, y'all gotta get disciplined."

"By who?" said Loco glaring at his young protégés.

"By us," Mike challenged.

These kids were all heading for a ass whooping, but it was Mike's big mouth that finalized it. Loco managed to grab John, Mike, and Big Head all at once, and pinned them on the ground. Crip Van trapped Kev and Lil Loco in a corner of the garage. The two Crips beat them something vicious. It was the old versus the young, but it wasn't much of a battle on the Wannabes behalf because they weren't as experienced as Loco and Crip Van. Needless to say they lost.

After the discipline, Crip Van capitalized on Kev's injury. Kev was still sore from his gun shot grazes and hadn't been much help during the battle. Crip Van pointed at Kev and said, "Aww, look at him, now that's fucked up! Y'all let Kev get y'all beat up and he didn't even help. I think he should be the one gettin' disciplined for leavin' y'all for dead. Not only that, but his stupid ass almost got killed yesterday by going into the Projects without any protection, so whose the one that needs a discipline?"

John shook his head and looked at Kev. They both knew what Van Crip meant. Kev balled his fist and leaned against the garage. His crew and his bestfriend had to discipline him.

John hated the entire process, but Kev took his disciple like a boss hog. There were no hard feelings between them, everyone had protocol. If Kev hadn't opened his big mouth in the first place he wouldn't have got into trouble, but it was in Kev's character to test the water.

After their tustle with Kev, the team went to work on the traps. However, Loco and Crip Van had other things on their minds.

NATURAL BORN KILLAZ

A few hours later, Loco watched Crip Van from inside the BMW, with two Uzis rested close by. Crip Van stood on the corner of Central and Vernon next to a pay phone. A short way from the corner sat "Diva's Plus" hair salon, which belonged to Shante. Shante was Meosha's uncle's wife and a renowned "gossip queen". The locals referred to her salon as "gossip city". Everybody knew, if you wanted to find out who was fucking who, who shot who, or who had money, all you had to do was ask at the salon.

To add even more interest, Shante was out of the Projects and her salon sat in Crip territory; that meant she didn't have much choice when it came to giving out information. Either give out or move out!

Crip Van stood by the pay phone until he saw a trifling looking sista enter the salon. He then made his move, running towards the salon and catching the closing door. Loco hopped out of the BMW, carrying both Uzis and ran in after him. He passed Crip Van one of the Uzis, and they laid the salon down.

With blue rags covering their faces cowboy style Loco yelled, "Y'all already know the drill, so er'body getta fuck down!"

Girls in the hood were known to carry pistols, so it was in Crip Van and Loco's best interest that the order was given, and all the women in the shop complied. All of them, except one pretty honey colored woman who defiantly sat in a salon chair.

"Bitch, get down!" barked Crip Van, as he grabbed her by the extensions that Shante had just put in her hair. The woman sprawled on the floor.

Shante groaned as she lay on her belly and hissed something. Loco heard the hiss, "Whachu say?"

"I said..." answered Shante raising her head. "I said, Black people can't neva do nothin' good without someone tryna bring us down..."

TERRY WROTEN

She paused, suddenly recognizing who was behind the blue rags. Shante was puzzled. "Why are these niggaz layin' my shop down", she thought, "Is it because what happened yesterday when Scottie and the twins shot that kid; or are they just tryna make my husband mad?"

Shante cautiously raised herself up on one elbow, "Loco, I know that's you and Van Crip, so why are y'all layin' down my shop? I haven't done anything to y'all!"

Shante was right. She often opened her door to them when they had been chased by the police. She even gave them information about the Bloods anytime they had needed it. She stayed sincere and tried to keep the peace, because it was in her best interests since her salon operated in their hood. Now Loco and Van Crip had bent the rules of gangbangin' and involved family, and that wasn't cool.

"You know what's dis all about," said Loco taking a step closer to her.

What Shante understood was that this was a serious situation and she was under threat; and at that moment it wasn't only her that was being threatened, but her salon was too. Loco knew she wouldn't give any information easily about Little Scottie or her husband. He saw the fear in her eyes and knew this was harsh, but it was the only way they were going to get what they wanted. He leaned over her, gun still pointed and said, "We aint gon' rob you or yo' clients. We just want information."

"Thank you Jesus!" the trifling looking girl sighed, "I just got my county check, and I don't need it taken. I gotta pay rent."

"Bitch, shut up!" Crip Van yelled. He was more aggressive than Loco and right now he had more reason to be mad, Kev was his brother and several of the women in the salon were the girlfriends of the Project Bloods. He bent over the trifling girl and pulled out

NATURAL BORN KILLAZ

several strands of her hair, "Bitch, were you plannin' to get those extensions done?"

Shante sighed. She knew Crip Van was trigger happy. She had watched him on many occasions shoot it out with the Bloods. Shante looked towards one of her clients named Sandra, hoping that she wouldn't open her mouth, but she could see that Sandra as usual was not going to shut up.

Shante frowned, "Sandra, please don't say nuthin'. Please!"

Loco started to clown around. He flexed his muscles and tapped Shante on the head with the Uzi, "Like I was sayin', we don't want y'all nasty pussy, money, y'all fake-ass jewelry, or y'all food stamps!"

The honey colored woman cut him off, "Hey, my pussy aint nasty! My jewelry ain't fake! And I'm not on the county!"

Crip Van was getting frustrated; the women were getting too bold. They were starting to play games.

"Bitch shut the fuck up!" he shouted as his Uzi sprayed a line of bullets across Shante's salon wall. In a matter of seconds, photos and pictures were lying in splintered heaps on the floor. The women screamed as flying debris hit them; the echoing bullets sent shock waves through the room.

"Shante!" yelled Crip Van, "Make dis bitch pay for what she said, since she like to talk so fuckin' much! And the next time some bitch interrupt, Imma put a hole in yo' ass!"

Loco kicked at a large piece of broken glass, sending it flying to smash against the counter, "Now look! Y'all makin' this harder than it has to be, so maybe y'all need a little encouragin'? Because if we don't get the information we want, we gon tear this muthafucka up! And since Miss Big Mouth Honey Cutie wants to talk so much, she's gon be the first to die. Then after her triflin' ass, Sandra gonna die! So let's make this easy." Shante felt the heat. She knew she was going to have to give them whatever they wanted.

TERRY WROTEN

She didn't want a murder in her shop, or the police interrogating her. "What is it?" she asked, "What do y'all want?"

Crip Van looked down at her as she laid on her stomach looking up at him. He knew that she was embarrassed. He didn't intend to wreak anymore havoc in her shop, as long as he got what he came for, Information.

"My fourteen year old brother, who don't gangbang, was almost gunned down by y'all folks yesterday. We all know how niggaz pillow talk, so I know somebody in this salon heard something. I want names!"

"I don't know nuthin', haven't seen nuthin', and ain't heard nuthin'!" said a middle aged woman with a towel wrapped around her head.

"I don't know either."

"Me too."

"Me three."

It appeared that none of the women knew anything, because they all denied any knowledge of the shooting. Loco and Crip Van found this very unlikely considering there were at least twenty women in the shop, a few women had to hear something. Gossip on the Eastside was known to spread like a transmitted disease.

"Cuzz!" Loco yelled. He had lost his temper, and the game was over. The women were playing him too close. As far as he was concerned there was no more if's, and's, or buts about it. He picked up a can of hair spray and threw it hard against a broken mirror. "Crip Van, kill that triflin' bitch on three," he pointed his Uzi in the direction of Sandra.

"One, two, thr..."

"Okay!" yelled Shante. "Okay! Please don't shoot!! I know who they are."

NATURAL BORN KILLAZ

Loco inwardly chuckled. Shante couldn't outsmart the fox. Loco had her right where he wanted, "So who are they?"

"Murda Dawg and Benzo," said Shante. "They are twins. They were with Scottie, they work for him. Scottie knew Kevin was related to y'all, so they tried to kill him. Kevin was walkin' my niece home. She came in the house cryin', she said that Scottie and the twins was tryna kill her boyfriend. My husband was hot but it was already too late. Them dumb niggaz had already did what they did. I even called the number Kevin gave Meosha, so my husband could talk to you on a man to man tip and apologize, but nobody answered. I knew this was gon' start a war. I just ask that y'all don't hurt my husband. I promise you, Red Flag didn't have anything to do with this."

Crip Van and Loco left the salon without any further damage.

Later that evening, Crip Van guided a stolen red Hyundai through the traffic like a torpedo, while Loco sat in the passenger seat bobbing his head to "187" by Dre and Eazy E. They were headed towards the Projects and murder was the only thing on their minds. When they arrived at Compton Avenue Loco turned down the music, "Stop cuzz," he said. "Put yo' rag on and check yo' Uzi. You know if any of these dudes see us its gon be all bad, and cuzz remember our course of action. It's gotta be in and out."

The Projects were deadly and infested with killers of all kind. Loco knew that by entering the Projects they were like flies trying not to get caught in a web, but they had planned an excellent strategy.

"What street did Shante say they be on?" he asked contemplating their next move. "We need to get straight to 'em, knock 'em down, and keep it movin'!"

Crip Van had a devilish grin on his face. He knew the Projects by heart. He was chased out of there so many times growing up, he knew more hideouts and catwalks than the Bloods. His first love Peaches, lived in the Projects and Crip Van took many chances to visit her. Peaches lived right in the heart of the Projects before she moved to Texas.

"Hey cuzz," he said. "I know exactly where they're at, and these dudes on this side are stupid! Watch."

Crip Van pulled up outside apartment #101. It was the unit Shante told them Scottie and his crew would be. Shante told them everything she knew in order to save her husband's skin, and she did not let them down. A crooked smirk grew across Loco's face when they pulled up and saw four Bloods shooting dice and hustling crack. With two Uzis, a drive-by shooting would have laid at least two of the four down, but that would have been too easy a kill. Plus the two reputable Crips wanted to make sure they got the three involved in Kev's shooting. One of the Bloods reached for his gun as they pulled up, but he was slow on the draw. Loco could have chopped him down, but decided to outsmart him.

"Hol' on, Lil' Homey! Its me, OG Brazy B off 33rd Street."

The young Bloods were fooled. They believed Loco and let their guard down. Loco and Crip Van had done their homework, by placing red rags over their mouth and nose and red fit-it hats on their heads that were turned backwards. Only their eyes were visible.

One of the Bloods immediately fell into their trap. "On Bloods," he said to the others. "That's Brazy B off 33rd Street." He was lying. He was trying to acknowledge status from his homies. It was obvious that he didn't know Brazy B, otherwise, he would not have been fooled.

Crip Van whispered, "These some dumb bastards."

Loco nodded in agreement.

"Ay, Blood," said Crip Van. "Where Scottie at?" He was pulling them in like fish caught in a net.

NATURAL BORN KILLAZ

One of the Bloods looked up from the dice game. "He aint here, Big Homie."

Those Bloods were so into that dice game, they took turns shooting dice, making five dollar sales and talking. They didn't even try to approach the car. It was obvious by looking at their body language that they were tuned in to the dice game.

Loco needed to get their full attention. "Who's running this spot?" he asked. "I need to know, because I got an important message for Scottie. I wanna give him and the other two little homies their props for what they did yesterday. I need to talk to Blood, because I need to know those homies names. They should move up in life. What they did was some straight up gansta shit."

Those Bloods may have been playing dice, but Loco played them like checkers, because they all started loosening up. The Blood, who had initially reached for his gun when Crip Van and Loco pulled up, was all smiles. "Oh, you talkin' 'bout that shit that happened on Compton?"

Loco nodded. "Yeah that's it." He tightened his grip around the Uzi as it sat on his lap. He felt his trigger finger itch, but he ignored the feeling. He wanted the Bloods to come closer towards the car and give him more information. And the young Blood holding the gun was so confident, he did just that. He was glad he had an important audience to brag about shooting at Kev. Here was Brazy B himself come to give him his well earned stripes. He ordered the others to hold the dice game and started walking towards the car. You could tell he was the leader of the pack.

"That shit that happened on Compton," he said moving closer to the car. "That was some shit me and my brother put down!"

Crip Van's mind exploded just thinking about the Blood standing a few feet away from the car bragging about how he nearly killed his little brother. Loco felt the tension building. He could hear Crip Van's breathing coming in short hard bursts. He knew and wanted every bullet to count, several of the Bloods were now moving very close towards the car, he turned to Crip Van and said "Cover yo' gun."

The confidant Blood drew closer. Loco leaned a little way out of the car window. "What you and yo' brother's names", he asked.

"I'm Murda Dawg and this…" he said indicating to a Blood on his left, "is my brother Benzo."

Loco forced a smile. "How old are y'all?"

"We just turned twenty the other day," he said.

Crip Van's breathing grew deeper and harder. The two puppets Scottie had used on his mission were brothers, and older than himself and Loco. All thoughts about his earlier plan, of kidnapping these dudes flew from his head. He had assumed that they would be younger around fourteen and a nice little trophy for John and his younger crew to deal with.

All the Bloods had surrounded the car. Crip Van leaned towards Loco and coarsely whispered, "Fuck 'em. Fuck the plan."

In a flick of a thumb, Loco read the murderous anticipation in Crip Van's voice. He tilted the passenger seat and moved to the back of the car. The Bloods were so dumb they didn't sense death, the game was almost over them. They had been fooled into thinking Loco was Brazy and like lambs they came to the slaughter.

"Oh shit! Some crab's!" Benzo yelled as the Uzi's came into play. His words cut to the bone as Crip Van blazed bullets on him and his brother.

Murda Dawg hit the ground first with his gun still in his waist band. In the back of the car, Loco sprayed bullets into everything that moved. In a matter of seconds four lives were gone. Crip Van and Loco knew the repercussions. This was war!

CHAPTER 6
BRAZY B

News traveled fast, Brazy B soon heard about the retaliation and he was hotter than fish grease. He walked into his Pasadena suburb house and slammed the door. He felt played. Word had reached him less than thirty minutes after his four soldiers were killed. Scottie had pulled up a few seconds after the shooting to find Murda Dawg crumpled and bleeding in the gutter. Still barely conscious, he told Scottie how they had been laid down. He died shortly after joining his brother and the rest of the crew.

Brazy B was angry as hell as he thought about his dead lil' homies. He was swearing death upon the Crips under his breath and thinking about the action he was going to take in retaliation as he walked into the living room. He yelled out to his girlfriend calling her name. At this moment, Brazy needed her. He not only needed her for comfort; he needed to instruct her on what he wanted her to do. He wanted her expertise as a snake and ghetto queen. He needed names and answers before he made any calls. He needed to know who to hit and he knew she was just the person to find out this information.

Sandra was a manipulator and an expert at uncovering the information that Brazy B needed. She was a pro at this. Beauty was not her only asset, she was a hoodrat, and one that any brother would be proud of. She had a certain swag about herself; and although

NATURAL BORN KILLAZ

ghettoified, Brazy B loved her. But most of all, he loved her loyalty towards him. She was his tamed snake. He yelled her name "Sandra!" and it echoed off every wall in the house. Sandra chose not to reply. Brazy knew she was somewhere in the house, so he called out to her again. It wasn't until the third time that Brazy called for her that she bothered to answer. "I'm in the room."

Brazy was mad. He swore under his breath as he climbed the stairs to the second floor of the house "Damn woman!" He angrily opened the bedroom door. The reddish-orange sun shone brightly on the pillows through the slats in the blinds. The glare and fire in his eyes told Sandra he was mad, and she knew it. Her knees started to tremble and her stomach fluttered as she turned off the video that she had been watching. She tried to smooth over the situation. "What's wrong?" "Are you hungry or something?"

"Naw, I'm not hungry. Murda Dawg and Benzo just got killed and the cats that did it played them with the oldest trick in the book. They used my name to wreck shop!"

Sandra was stun. She couldn't believe her ears. She knew exactly who had killed them. Her gut feeling told her that it was the two Crips that had laid Shante's salon down. She thought for a moment then clicked her fingers 'Loco and Crip Van were their names'. When they had terrorized Shante and her clients they had been talking as if Lil' Scottie and his boys were in for it. Sandra was one hundred percent sure it was them and she felt bad for not mentioning the incident to Brazy B.

"Baby," she whispered "I've got something to tell you." Her eyes filled with tears as she spoke.

Brazy saw that she was distressed and asked "Blood, what wrong? Why you cryin?"

Sandra wiped her face with a Kleenex as Brazy sat on the bed next to her. She shook her head. "I know who killed 'em."

Brazy was amazed at how fast word of the killings had got around. He sighed, "Damn! It's on the streets already?"

"No," Sandra replied, "It's not on the streets. It's a long story; so let me tell you."

Sandra told Brazy about the incident that had happened in Shante's salon and how Loco and Crip Van had laid the shop down. But she changed half of the story. Sandra was good at fabricating.

"Baby, them niggas even took my food stamps. They emptied my shoppin' bag and took everything. And after they stuck their guns in my mouth, Shante gave them the information they wanted so they wouldn't kill me. Then, they said 'fuck yall slob bitches' and ran out of the salon. I know its them because they said, they were gon kill anyone who even look like a Blood."

Brazy knew that Sandra was stretching the truth. She always did! What part of the story was true and what was a lie, Brazy didn't know so he decided to take every word as gospel. He had heard about the incident of Scottie and his boys shooting at the young wannabe Crip, and he had been real hot about it. Brazy didn't believe in foul play or involving innocent family members into a fight that was suppose to be kept on the streets. Scottie was going to get some serious discipline for the stunt that he had pulled, but since Loco and Crip Van had retaliated Brazy was going to go and get them first.

In the hood, everyone has to live by the unspoken law (by any means that are deemed necessary), so Brazy B was inflicting the law as he set his mind to murder.

CHAPTER 7

May 22nd, 1994

It was Saturday, John and his crew had just worked the spots that Killa had organized for them to work. After work, he and Kev took Donita and Meosha to the skating rink and then to the movies. The girls wanted to go shopping after the movies so they did just that and everything in style. Killa had let John borrow the Lexus like he'd promised. The car was top notch and the rims shone brightly reflecting in the passing shop windows. Kev and the girls were impressed with the wheels and John head began to grow big as a bimp. He just knew he was the man.

John was in love and Killa was more than pleased. Killa figured, having Donita at John's side was a bonus; it would keep his mind off the streets and wanting to become a gang member. Plus, the war between the Crips and the Bloods was growing stronger every passing day; and at night the drive-by's became more frequent.

During the week, Kev arrived at John's house every morning at seven o'clock. From there, they'd walk to school. The walk was short as Carver was only around the corner. That particular Monday morning Kev was like the cat who swallowed the cream and he taught John. John was heated because he'd lost a bet with Kev over a game between the Supersonics and the Lakers. They agreed that the loser would have to carry everyone's books for the whole the semester, and that included Donita's and Meosha's as well as Kev's.

NATURAL BORN KILLAZ

"Here you go player," said Kev pushing a pile of books towards John.

John looked at him sideways and frowned, "Cuzz, I know you aint gon really make me carry yo' books. Are you?"

Kev raised his eyebrows. "It was you who tried to be a smart ass. You know the business."

John looked at him and knew he was done. He had lost a fair bet so he sighed, "I'll carry 'em." He kicked his foot hard against a picket fence and swore loudly to himself. He knew he was acting like a sore loser.

Kev shrugged but he could sense John's anger. He started laughing, "Ha!Hey, stop actin' like a ho'."

"Whachu say?" John yelled snatching his two math books out of his hands.

Kev, sensing John's rising anger, put his hand on his shoulder, "Nigga, only ho's work with feelings."

Sometimes Kev knew John better than he knew himself, but he didn't let his boy off lightly. He waited until they walked almost all the way to school before he said, "Cuzz, dry those eyes, you don't gotta carry my books, and you don't gotta carry my girl's either."

John grinned. He was lost for words. Kev was giving him a pass on the bet, so he handed him back his books and said, "Good lookin' Crip."

Kev just nodded.

Donita and Me-Me were awaiting their arrival. When they arrived at the front entrance the two girls were caught off guard when they grabbed for their books. Me-Me pulled away saying, "Aww hell to the naw!" Me-Me was in one of her ghetto moods. She didn't like the fact that Kev had obviously reneged on his bet and was disappointed because there would be no opportunities for her and Donita to taught John. Kev looked Me-Me up and down from head to toe and said, "Aww hell to the naw what? As long as yo' books are carried girl, you shouldn't have a problem."

You could see the bond that had grown between Kev and Me-Me since Kev's shooting and he was trying to educate her away from the coarse ghetto talk and attitude. Kev pointed a finger towards her. "Didn't I tell you about being ghetto? That shit don't look pretty."

Miss Phillips smiled when Donita and John walked into homeroom holding hands. She liked the fact that they were together. Miss Phillips was so proud of their union she went about promoting them as *the strong young black couple.* Everyone in school knew about Donita and John mainly from Miss Phillips promotion, but he and Kev did their own promoting at nutrition time. They walked around the school holding hands with the girls and everybody, even Mr. Rudy couldn't help but notice the pretty couples.

After school, Miss Phillips stood at the front entrance while Donita and John stood nearby awaiting the crew. Miss Phillips looked at John with so much happiness in her eyes. She smiled, giving her silent approval. Most people thought the situation between Donita and John was positive. John couldn't help but smile back, showing Miss Phillips his happiness. Miss Phillips was becoming the most respected teacher in the school; even Kev was beginning to like her. She smiled again and slapped her wrist, indicating that she was watching John and that he better not do anything to get a spanking. Miss Phillips was real special to John and through his adolescent eyes she was just like a big homegirl.

When the whole crew arrived, John waved to Miss Phillips. She waved back as they mobbed off.

At Jack-in-the-Crack, Kev and John bought two strawberry milkshakes. They all hung in the restaurant for a while, but the manager kicked them out after Popa bought in all his elementary friends to hang out with the older crowd. Popa's friends were a bad mob and

NATURAL BORN KILLAZ

combined with John's boys they were over fifteen deep. The manager was cool with John and his crew, but Popa's crew already had a reputation. They were the definition of Bay Bay Kids.

They left Jack-in-the-crack and headed for the block, only to be told by Crip Van and Loco that there was going to be no hanging out. Kev, John and the girls decided to lock ourselves in Miss Goodman's house. Having the house to themselves created the perfect opportunity for Kev and John to try their luck. Kev took Meosha into his room and tried to take her virginity, but she wasn't ready. In the living room, Donita shot John down like Queen Latifah in that movie *Set It Off*.

She said "I knew you were going to try and get you some as soon as we were alone. I love you John, but I'm not ready for you to take my virginity."

John chuckled. Donita hit it right on the nose, John was trying to do just that; and that day he saw his virginity stay right where it was; intact.

He said "Even though I'm devastated from being turned down, I'm not hurt because, in all honesty, I need some more advise about sex from Killa."

Donita and John were growing closer; their feelings becoming emotional, so he needed a little help from his brother.

Time slipped away from them on that day and a few hours later Kev came running into the living room. "Cuzz it's time to go! Mom's on her way home."

Donita and John were still making out when Kev came flying in like a bat out of hell. John frowned, "Cuzz, you a salt shaker."

"Cuzz, nobody gotta hate on you," Kev said heatedly. "We just gotta fuckin' go befo' moms gets here."

John looked at the clock, Miss Goodman and Mama would be on their way home, so he ans Kev left (walking Donita and Me-Me home as far as they could). Since the girls lived in different directions, Hooper was the turn off point (street) where they kissed and said "goodbye".

The two wannabes hurried back home after reaching Hooper. Hooper was only three main streets over from the block, but it spelt danger!

As they walked home, Kev bragged about his long term plans with Meosha. "John, watch! Me and Meosha gon' get married, have three kids, and move outta the hood."

John agreed. "Yeah, me too! But my kids with Donita gon' be smart, have er'thing they want and gon' be hustlaz."

Kev smiled. This was the first time they'd ever talked about their future in a positive way. Hanging with Donita and Meosha was changing a lot of negative aspects about them. For the first time, they weren't narrowing themselves to the true blue. They were starting to see things in different shapes, forms and colors. However, life in the hood was not going to be that simple; for every positive step there was always going to be negative steps to set them back in the hood.

Later that night, John heard gun fire but he didn't budge. He had grown up with the sounds of gun shots. He was more interested in catching some sleep; a drive-by in Los Angeles was nothing new to him and the norm. He'd just fell asleep when Mama's screaming woke him. "My baby!"

"My baby!!"

"My baby!!!"

John hopped out of bed like a cadet in military boot camp and ran into the living room. He couldn't believe his eyes upon seeing Mama. "What happened?" were the only words he could muster as the shock waves hit him. Mama's white gown was covered in blood and she couldn't stop crying. John knew something terrible had happened to one of his brothers. He could smell death.

Hot scalding tears streamed down John's face. He grabbed Mama by her bloodied nightgown sobbing. "What happened Mama? What happened?"

Mama's body shook with grief. She clutched John and in her eyes he saw death. "It's Bernard! Bernard and Van are dead!!"

The air seemed to grow thicker. John could barley breath as he ran outside. When he reached the porch, he saw his brother Loco stretched out, in the middle of the street, with Jasmine kneeling over him. She was yelling and slapping his cheek.

"Bernard get up! Bernard, for God's sake, get up!!"

Bernard never got up. He was dead! He had been shot in the head. John's body now convulsed with involuntary shudders. He looked at the pool of blood his brother was lying in and knew this would be my last memory of Loco.

Further along the street, sprawled out on the sidewalk, was the lifeless body of Crip Van with his gun still clutched firmly in his hand. His upper torso was riddled with bullets. By the way the scene unfolded, John's gut feeling told him Loco and Crip Van were set up. The block had been secured with strict regimentation and was tighter than Fort Knox, so it was obvious that the deaths were an inside job. Someone had fucked up!

The LAPD had taken their time in arriving to the scene, and time went slowly. It seemed an hour or more passed before they finally arrived. White sheets were placed over Loco and Crip Van, and they both were declared dead on arrival. Tears of frustration and anger poured down John's face when Detectives Gilbert and Gilmore pulled up at the scene. They were as corrupt as rotting garbage and they smiled at each other, knowing the murders were gang related. They loved seeing Crips and Bloods kill each other. In their opinion, the cases were easy to solve because it didn't matter who they convicted, innocent or guilty. It didn't matter at all, as long as a "nigger" was incarcerated. Their motto was 2 for 1: one dead and one behind bars.

John's tears would not stop flowing and the lump in his throat grew threatening to choke him. As he sat through the night with Kev, they sat like zombies on the curb in front of their houses and watched the police clean up the crime scene. Their emotions were raw with grief and as they sat on that curb, they talked about their brothers and how they were going to miss them. Crip Van had been Kev's idol, so he turned to John and said, "Man, I love you. Cuzz, you my nigga. If anything ever happened to you, I'll go crazy. So imma tell you this, for Loco and my brother imma kill some slobs. And that's on Crip!"

John looked at his best friend and even though he was emotional, he knew Kev was serious. Kev was making plans; ones that he intended to carry out. John put his arm around Kev's shoulder, "Cuzz, I feel that. And even if Donita's brothers were involved, imma kill them too."

John and Kev sat on that curb for a long time planning revenge before they were interrupted by Jazz. She was holding the cordless house phone and still crying, "John, telephone."

John got up from the gutter and looked at his sister. He felt fresh hot tears burning in his eyes, and then they began to roll down his cheeks. He never saw Jasmine cry a day in his life. She was hurt. Loco had been her backbone, and John felt her pain. Crying, he hugged her before he grabbed the phone.

He cleared his throat and said, "Hello" into the phone.

Killa was on the end of the line. He told John he was safe and calling to make sure that he was alright. John sensed Killa was drained, he knew he had to be man of the family, even if it was only temporary. Shit, truth be told, Killa was going through

NATURAL BORN KILLAZ

grief as well. Killa told John he was out handling business, and needed him and Kev to take care of Mama, Jasmine, Miss Goodman, and Popa. After hanging up, John and Kev tried to do what Killa had asked of them, but they couldn't. They never experienced death so close in their families, and it was eating them alive. It was even harder for John to witness his mother cry. Mama was a very strong woman, so it was seldom that people seen her cry. The more she cried, the more John felt the urge for revenge.

All night the same thoughts turned over and over in John's head, "Did Brazy B or Bay Bay have anything to do with the killings?"

John couldn't accept the fact that whoever shot his brother had done so at point blank range. Loco got smoked! If Brazy B or Bay Bay had anything to do with the murders, it was going to spoil John's relationship with Donita. He knew one thing for sure, somebody was going to die! Loco's death changed his life forever.

On that fateful night, the beast within him was fighting to escape. John felt the urge to kill, and so did Kev.

CHAPTER 8

KILLA

May 23rd, 1994

Loyalty and respect were the only two words that hit every wall in the basement of Killa's Marina Del Rey house. The basement was the spot where all major gatherings took place. It was furnished with a large mahogany table with matching chairs, giant pool table, miniature bar, big screen television, and a wall adorned with collector's item guns. It was the place only reputable members knew about, and often where members paid for their wrong doings.

John knew it was an inside job that caused the deaths of Loco and Crip Van. John knew it the moment he'd seen Loco stretched out in a pool of blood that somebody had slipped. It didn't take Killa long to find the weakest link, and he immediately identified the culprit as a snake, which was worse than an enemy.

The man in the hot seat was Crip Charlie, and he was in the basement strapped butt naked to the pool table while Ebony, Midnight, and two young Westside Crips named Crazoe and Midget stared at Killa. They all anticipated murder. Crip Charlie had become nothing but a traitor and a goon to everyone gathered in that room; a gangsta that had turned bitch. Everyone knew his future status; he was soon going to be as dead as a doorknob.

Killa had been betrayed. He was hurt and as he leaned over the object of his frustration he said, "Nigga, how could you just say fuck the hood and expect to live? Nigga, you know we live and die

NATURAL BORN KILLAZ

by the G-code. Nigga, how dare you?! How dare you help the Bloods kill two of our solders? And my lil' brothers at that..."

Crip Charlie cut Killa off. He was in a real bad situation and tried to plead for his life, "Killa, listen to me. It wasn't like..."

Ebony aimed her balled fist and struck hard against his face. His words were cut abruptly short as three loud smacks echoed around the room.

Smack.

Smack.

Smack.

"Shut the fuck up you bitch," Ebony hissed, "Speak only when you are told too."

Charlie knew Ebony was deadly, so he complied with her orders. He knew she was Killa's Bonnie, and Killa was her Clyde. They shared an unspoken motto "anything outrageous equals death." Sensing Charlie's growing weakness and fear, Ebony asked Killa if she could torture him. Killa was silent, as he stood over Charlie with tears in his eyes. He looked down at the man spread eagle and shook his head in disbelief. Ebony seeing the pain in her lover's eyes begged him to let her do what she saw fit.

"Baby, since he like gettin' his dick sucked while the Bloods are killin' my brothers, you should let me suck his dick too." Ebony chuckled as she grabbed Charlie's dick by the shaft and punched him in the balls. Charlie groaned and she pulled out her blade.

Killa nodded in agreement as she went to work, deciding to let her have her revenge.Charlie's pleas for mercy came in agonizing bursts, as Killa questioned him about slippin' and the consequences leading up to the murders of Loco and Crip Van.

Crazoe and Midget learned a lesson that night; a lesson that taught them how deadly females could be. Midnight sat quietly observing. He believed in the saying "each one teach one." He had taught Killa the game and the codes of the streets and in turn Killa had taught Ebony. Now, purely by her sadistic action Ebony taught Cazoe and Midget.

Charlie withered and screamed in agony as Killa held up his hand indicating for the torture to stop, "I think Charlie will tell the whole truth now. Isn't that right, Charlie?"

Ebony frowned as she wiped the blood off her blade, "too bad we can't call you Crip Charlie any more. Yousa fuckin' sell out."

Midnight and Killa's eyes met and they smiled knowingly, Ebony had grown over the years into a true gangsta diva.

Killa turned his attention back to Charlie, "I said, isn't that right?"

Tiny beads of sweat trickled down Charlie's petrified face. He looked at Killa and nodded his head in agreement. It was time to revisit the not so distant past that now seemed to be a lifetime away.

~~~~~~

The LAPD were on a mission! They were enforcing the new *three strikes law* and cracking down on drug distribution. Their raids came thick and fast, crawling over every hot spot in the ghetto, ultimately shutting elicit drug dealers down. In order to keep the money flowing for the Crips, Killa set up shop on the block and tightened security, insisting that nobody hangout. The police had become fed up, and were handing out life sentences hand over fist.

Mama's house was in the middle of the block, so Killa set up his structure around her house. Loco, Crip Van, and Crip Charlie worked the seven to seven shift on the block. Loco positioned himself outside Mama's house with five ounces of crack concealed in his jacket. He planned to sell those five ounces first, while Crip Van and Charlie both served as security.

There was a security post set up on each corner of the block, which held a walkie-talkie and Uzi. Each post had served a specific purpose. With a house on each corner posing as a security post, it was almost impossible for the police to stop the hustle. It also served as a fool-proof safety seal against rival gangs committing homicides.

As Crip Charlie sat on the porch of his designated security house, his walkie-talkie went off. He was smoking a blunt at the time and as he picked up the gadget, he heard Crip Van saying, "Watch that white Datson turnin' on yo' end." Charlie hopped up and put out the blunt. He grabbed his Uzi and approached the car. The driver, one step ahead of him got out and tried to move the signs that read *Street Closed.*

Street signs were placed in the middle of the street every night after ten; they were used to keep traffic down during the early hours of the morning. Charlie looked at the driver; a vanilla sister and pointed his Uzi directly at her face. He was using smart street tactics. When he got a few feet away from the car he asked, "Who else is in that bucket?" He stood ridged, anticipating the slightest movement. Any movement in the car would have spelled ambush, so Charlie used precaution.

The vanilla trifling looking sister casually stepped back into the car saying, "Nobody." Charlie moved closer to the two door Datson and cautiously looked in. Satisfied, it was clear he relaxed saying, "So who are you lookin' for?"

Looking up at him she smiled sweetly, "Marcel. I'm looking for Marcel. I met him at Roscoes and this is the street he told me to meet him on. I hope he didn't give me the wrong address, because I was plannin' to give his fine ass some pussy."

The word pussy bought an instant smile to Charlie's face. He thought "Damn, I got me one". He decided it was in his best interest to shoot game, "Boo, I think, that nigga gave you the wrong address, because don't no Marcel live on this block. But if you wanna

TERRY WROTEN

holla at a real nigga, holla at me."

The sister licked her lips and smiled. Crip Charlie was a little boy in her eyes, "Little boy, please! You too young for this hot stuff right here."

Charlie blushed. He tried to reply but his mouth tripped over his tongue, amused at his apparent lack of sophistication she laughingly went on. "Little boy, I'll suck your dick so good you'll be seein' dots."

Crip Charlie froze. This sister was more aggressive than he had anticipated. He started bulging through his pants and his other head started doing the thinking. He said, "Damn! Like that?"

"Yep," the sister replied. "They don't call me Diamond for nothin'. I swear I'll have yo' young ass seein' thangs…"

The sudden interruption of Crip Van's voice on the walkie-talkie pulled Charlie back into reality, "hey, what's happening?"

Snapping out of the spell, Charlie realized that he was slippin'. He was in the middle of the street with his Uzi in his right hand and the walkie-talkie in the left. He had been thinking about pleasure before business, instead of business before pleasure.

He turned towards Diamond and said, "Look peep game Diamond, a nigga gotta get back to work. Right now, I'm grindin' and the homies aint with this, so wantchu shoot me yo' number and we'll take it from there."

Diamond smiled. She liked Charlie's catch line, "I have a better idea. Why don't I just come back in twenty minutes and park around the corner? That way yo' boys don't see me. I know I sound crazy, but I was hoping to get some dick from Marcel's fine ass. Since I can't get any from him, you will have to do. And to be honest I'm not from these parts, I'm from the Valley, but I like gangsta niggaz. So if you want, I'll come back."

NATURAL BORN KILLAZ

"Damn! This bitch really want some dick," Charlie thought becoming aroused again. 'What's wrong with a lil' head, if nobody knows she's here?'

The hunger in Charlie's eyes gave Diamond the answer she was looking for.

"I'll be back," she purred as she turned towards her Datson swaying her hips in a tantalizing motion that made Charlie rise like yeast. She had the body and face of a goddess. She drove away and he ran back to the porch.

As he settled himself on the porch, Crip Van's voice cut through the airwaves, "What was that? Is er'thing straight?"

Charlie put his lips to the speaker, "Yeah, er'thing straight. I was just holla'n at some bitch from the Valley called Diamond. A nigga might have some pussy lined up for later."

"A'ight cuzz, but Loco got one mo' ounce to sell, then it's yo' turn, so stay posted."

Charlie put his walkie-talkie down next to him. He sat and watched the block while taking pulls off his blunt. "Damn," he thought as she came into view. Diamond was back sooner than he had anticipated.

"This bitch really came back," he said softly to himself. He knew she couldn't see him from the angle he was sitting, so he stood up and walked over to the gate in the yard, unlocked it and said, "Come on in."

Diamond was trifling and she knew it, but she was a thoroughbred and so beautiful Charlie could not resist her. Even with her brazen demeanor, he had to possess her. From the way she flaunted her body he could detect the snake in her, but he was too hypnotized and had succumbed to her seductive walk and talk.

"Come on," she said. "Let's get this over with. I had to come back early because I got a call and have to get back to the Valley. I didn't want to leave you hangin' so I came right back," That was a lie.

Charlie's hunger did not see through Diamond's cunning ways as he said, "A'ight, come on. Don't trip."

The side of the house was the only place they could go, since Killa was paying the tenants to use only the porch as a station. Killa was more than generous, not only paying the two fine sisters who lived in the station houses for their front porch, but he had also bought them new cars and gave them dick when Ebony wasn't around. So inside the houses were off limits to his workers.

Diamond wasted no time on the side of the house. She unfastened Charlie's 501's and got busy. She gave blows to Charlie's head like knock out punches from Tyson in the 80's. She was so talented that his eyes rolled to the back of his head, and he didn't notice the signal she gave her three accomplices. The Bloods disguised as bums pushing baskets crept right past Charlie. They could have killed him, but they had bigger fish to fry. He posed no threat; Diamond already had him by the balls.

Charlie slipped!

When he nutted and had come back to his senses, he heard Van Crip yelling through the walkie-talkie, "Charlie!"

"Charlie! Why did you let these smokers on the block with their baskets?"

"Oh shit," Charlie thought pushing Diamond away. He swallowed hard knowing he had slipped big time. He ran to the porch and grabbed his walkie-talkie, but it was too late shots started echoing around the block, and his nostrils filled with the acidic smell of gun smoke. He raced to the middle of the street just in time to see Crip Van being gunned down. Like a film in slow motion, he watched the sparks fired from Van's Uzi vanish in a cloud of smoke, as he slowly crumbled to the ground.

NATURAL BORN KILLAZ

His breathing became harder and faster as he noticed Loco's lifeless body stretched out in the middle of the street. He ran down the block with his Uzi blazing and his lungs screaming for air. He kept running and shooting long before he realized his clip was empty, as he desperately attempted to shoot at least one of the Bloods.

However, it was too late, the Bloods and Diamond got away!

He suddenly stopped. Shock overpowered his body. He began to shake, and his arms and legs felt like they were weighed down with steal. He knew that he had fucked up and was the cause of the bloodshed that confronted him. He knew he had to get away.

Fate dealt a double hand that day.

Cazoe and Midget, traveling eastbound from the Westside were on the same frequency as the Eastside Crips. They were three blocks away when the drama unfolded, and they had heard all the drama through the walkie-talkies.

Crazoe yelled, "Fuck!" as he accelerated his foot flat on the pedal.

When he and Midget turned the corner to the crime scene, they saw Crip Charlie getting into his car.

Crazoe leaped from the car they were traveling in and pulled out his 357, "nigga where yo' bitch ass goin'? We heard er'thing! And you made a deadly mistake. You slipped!"

~~~~~~~

Charlie's breathing was now shallow; it was as if all the life had suddenly been expelled from his body. Killa had paced around the pool table listening to Charlie's side of the story. His face lined in thought, complicating the rightful punishment for his fallen soldiers. It hurt knowing that Charlie had been his protégé. It hurt that this man had been adorned with ranks that were obviously given without due forth sight. But it was perfectly clear that this man had made a deadly mistake. A mistake that had cost two Crips their lives and now he was to pay the penance: his own life was up for taking.

Killa thought long and hard. Loyalty was something this man did not have. His dick was more important than the Crips. Respect was not on his agenda. He went against protocol. The man said, "fuck the rules" ultimately putting everyone's life in jeopardy.

Killa saw hustling as an art, so death before betrayal was his only conclusion. Even though Killa had thought of every possible way of overlooking the consequences, he still came to the same conclusion: Charlie had to go to the sharks.

He stopped pacing and addressed the audience, "Do we the jury find Charlie guilty of violating the G-code, death before dishonor? All in favor of the death penalty, say I."

The basement filled with resounding I's. Charlie closed his eyes awaiting death. The amount of pain he suffered at a snake's hand was a relief, when his final moments were relieved by Ebony slicing open his throat.

Killa shook his head sadly as Charlie died. He'd never dreamt that he would have to be in the position of ordering a Crip's death, especially not Charlie's. He gave instructions to Crazoe and Midget to dispose of the body, and told Ebony to clean up her mess.

"When er'thing is done, y'all meet me and Midnight on the Eastside. It's going down."

CHAPTER 9

When the sun rose in the morning neither John or Kev were worried about attending school. They had made up their minds that they would not go back until the madness with their brothers had evened out. They were sitting on the front porch contemplating their next move, when Killa arrived with over a hundred Crips following him. They had come from all over. C-R-I-P was written all over the block. Blue rags, blue hats, blue belts, blue khakis, and blue Chuck Taylors flooded the street. The OGs, BGs, and TGs swarmed onto the block like a mosquito plague. Killa led the pack, and made it clear that the Bloods were responsible for the slayings. The only and major problem he faced was lack information about which Blood sect had crossed the line to commit murder, so he ordered a hit on every Blood sect in Los Angeles.

John listened intently as Killa gave his speech. The hurt over Loco's death was still gaping like an open wound, John admired the support and respect the Crips were showing, and his inspiration for officially becoming a Crip arose. He looked at Kev as the Crips gathered together and said, "Kev, it's about time."

Kev glanced at John with a puzzled look, "about time for what?"

"It's about time we started bangin' this Crip shit for real."

NATURAL BORN KILLAZ

Kev made eye contact with John and saw that he was dead serious. He cracked a one-sided smile and said, "Well let's go holla at Killa."

Killa wasn't impressed with their plans. He just lost one little brother and Crip Van to the streets. There wasn't anything positive in gangbangin' and he made it very clear about the risks involved. In the end, he left the choice up to John and Kev, because he knew once a kid made their mind up to become a gangsta, there was no stopping them. They chose to join, and he chose to guide them through the process.

"Man," he said. "I love yall and gon' ride with y'all decision, but I'm seriously hurt. Man, this ain't the life to live…"

"Come on Killa," Kev intervened, "Stop actin' like we some punks or somethin'."

Killa frowned, "A'ight! Since y'all being hard headed, let me get some homies to put y'all on."

The noise level had grown to a crescendo during the conversation, and now Killa turned towards the large gathering of Crips and shouted, "Excuse me!"

"Excuse me!" Gaining their attention he proceeded. "First off, I wanna thank all of you for comin' out and supportin' me, my family, and the homie Crip Van's family. However, before we go do our gangsta thang, my lil' brothas wanna get put on the sect. I need a few tiny gangstas to put these Locs on. They're only fourteen, so I need some TGs around their age."

Crazoe was seventeen at the time and a rising General; he looked John up and down saying, "I'll put the tall one on by myself." He then called John to the middle of the street.

John frowned, he wasn't afraid of Crazoe. Shit, this was a perfect opportunity to gain instant strikes amongst the other ranking Crips. He eyed Crazoe up and down and was about to say, "fool whatever," but Midnight cut him off.

"Crazoe, you're too old for young cuzz."

Crazoe only stood two inches taller than John, and they weighed about the same. John decided to defend himself; he didn't need Midnight's concern. He was a gangsta by nature. He said, "Cuzz, I'll fight Crazoe and whoever else wanna jump in. This Crip here!"

Killa held up his hand up in protest. It was his turn to cut John off. He knew Crazoe was the best fighter out of all the young Crips and he didn't want to see his younger brother get demolished, "Aww hell naw nigga! You aint 'bout to fight Crazoe!"

"Come on, man," John pleaded with Killa. He knew fighting Crazoe could instantly earn him rank. Crazoe was the next Lieutenant-General in line since the deaths of Loco and Crip Van, and John felt a burning need to take over where his brother left off. He was from the Eastside and Crazoe was from the West. He would have been a "rat's ass," if he would have allowed Crazoe to come on his side of town, call him out, and not take the challenge. He begged Killa to allow him to fight Crazoe, and in the end he got his way.

"Fuck it! Nigga, you betta not lose seeing how you want to fight this nigga so bad!"

Before the fight Kev looked at John with a sinister grin. There was never a fair fight when it came to John and his crew. They were like the Musketeers: all for one and one for all. John knew that Kev would jump-in regardless of the outcome, so he chuckled inwardly thinking, "Yeah you bitch-ass niggaz tryna come on the Eastside and start shit, I got some tricks fo'dat ass."

Butterflies unleashed themselves in John's stomach as he walked to the middle of the street. It wasn't so much fear as it was anxiousness. He knew Crazoe was an excellent fighter. As they squared off he relaxed. Underestimating John, Crazoe began to showoff by jumping around and imitating Muhammad Ali. Crazoe figured

NATURAL BORN KILLAZ

John to be an easy victory, but boy was he wrong.

John was glad Crazoe thought of him as an easy fight. He eventually got bored with all the jumping around and fancy moves, so he threw a hard right hook but missed. Crazoe snapped out of his trance and his eyes sprang wide open. He looked stunned from John's bold move and answered with a hard left. Ducking the punch, John counter attacked with a two piece that connected with Craoze's jaw. His adrenaline rushed as he stepped in with lighting and landed speed left-right combination. Crazoe lost his balance as the punches connected with his jaw and collapsed. He jumped back as Crazoe hit the ground. He stood in his fighting stance waiting to get ram packed. He was amped up, and Midnight didn't make the situation any better, "Dayuum! Little cuzz fucked Crazoe up!!"

A big smile spread across John's face and out the corner of his eye, he saw Midget frowning. Sensing he was about to say something, John laughed.

Heated from the outcome, Midget turned towards Kev and said, "Cuzz now you gotta see me."

With a flick of the wrist, Kev answered his request.

Smack!

Smack!

Smack!

Kev hit Midget with three blows so savage it made John think twice about ever messing with Kev and mumble, 'Damn!' to himself.

John admired the way Kev handled his business. Kev was the same height as Midget, but Midget had three years more experience as a fighter. John was elated by the show he and Kev put on. Kev threw a combination of left, right, right, left on Midget; but just as John was smiling inwardly all hell broke loose! The Westside boys had become edgy. It all became too much seeing both

TERRY WROTEN

Crazoe and Midget beaten. They attacked Kev from behind. Their initiation turned into five against two, but Kev and John stood their ground. It was a miracle when Donita and Me-Me stepped into the picture, almost as if greater forces were at work.

As they fought Donita and Me-Me joined in throwing punches and yelling, "Get off our boyfriends!"

It was their brave move that made Killa and the other Crips break up the fight. John's adrenaline was rushing. He was mad that he and Kev got rushed in their own territory. There was a bruise on the top of his forehead, and Kev had a busted nose. John shook his head snarling out loud, "Damn! I wish my crew was here!"

He and Kev were on edge, contemplating whether to rekindle the fire by rushing Crazoe and his crew. It was hard to accept the fact they were jumped on their own block and they didn't like it one bit. To them, it was intolerable but they had made a choice and this was the outcome of joining a gang, so they had to accept it.

After everything had mellowed out, Donita was curious to know why they missed school. She also wanted to know why they were fighting. John shrugged his shoulders, but Donita wasn't stupid. She knew what was taking place; she just wanted justification why he was joining the Crips. He almost choked on his words as he told her, "The Bloods killed my brother and Crip Van last night."

Donita's eyes filled with tears as the force of John's words registered; she knew things would never be the same. When it came to the Red and the Blue, the world had already separated them and things were bound to change for the worst. Donita's voice was shaking, "John, we both know what this gon lead too, so do you want me to leave? I love you, but maybe we won't survive this?"

Looking at Donita, John could see the fear and frustration in her eyes. He put his hands on her shoulders and drew her closer to him. "No girl, don't leave! I need to holla at you about some real stuff,

NATURAL BORN KILLAZ

but first I gotta handle my business. So you and Meosha go wait at my house."

The next step of their initiation was to retrieve some source of protection and secure their street names. In Los Angeles, popping a cap was fundamental, so security came in the form of guns. Guns to them were like the Bible to a devoted Christian or the Qu'ran to a Muslim. They had to have one to survive, where the jungle creed must feed. A gangsta without a pistol was like a referee without a whistle. As Killa handed them their first guns, Kev couldn't believe his eyes. They were given identical .22s,

"Dayuuum! Killa good lookin!"

Killa smiled, "Yall gonna need 'em."

The smile on John's face spread from ear to ear, as he flipped his new piece in the palm of his hand. He tried his best not to look at Killa. He knew even though Killa had allowed the initiation to go down, he wasn't feeling good about it.

"John you know you have put me in a fucked up situation. We've talked about this on many occasions, but since this is what you want to do, I'm here for you."

John felt bad, he had never gone against Killa. Kev on the other hand was acting as if it wasn't a big deal, but Killa's words were still ringing in his ears. What was done was done. However, that didn't stop Killa from going on, "Look! Since this is what y'all wanna do, y'all gon' be under me and nobody else. We gon' call you Little Killa," he said pointing to John. "And Kev gon' be called Killa Kev. Since I can't keep y'all from hangin' out, we gotta come up with a plan for y'all and your crew."

John knew exactly what Killa meant. He knew Killa wanted them to stay in school, even if were gangbang. John liked the idea of being named after his big brother, but he also wanted to keep his own name. He told Killa, "I'll be Little Killa, but imma push 'Killa Black'."

TERRY WROTEN

Kev laughed,"Ha!"

"Yeah cuzz, imma be Killa Kev only after I kill a slob."

Killa chuckled, their responses stunned him. He shook his head saying, "Well tonight, imma take yall to get that Killa title."

John and Kev both nodded, and agreed by saying, "a'ight!

~~~~~~~

John was surprised when he and Kev walked into Mama's house. Donita and Meosha were engaged in an in-depth conversation with Mama and Miss Goodman, smiling from ear to ear, and gossiping with them like nothing was wrong. John smiled at Mama and her smile immediately turnned to a frown. He knew she wanted to say something to him but she seemed at a lost for words. Jasmine however, beat her to the chase, "John, whatta fuck is wrong witchu? Just tell me why you and Kevin went and did some crazy shit?"

Jasmine was still in her room grieving when John had initially walked in, but she soon made her presence felt. Jasmine was hurt and mad with grief over Loco's killing, and here John was being stupid enough to follow in his footsteps. By the look on her face, John knew that she wanted to haul off and beat the crap out of him. She was only two inches shorter than him, but packed a powerful punch. Meeting her gaze, he could almost see Loco staring at him with those blazing eyes, she had his flare. A shiver ran down his spine, he didn't know what to say. She silenced everyone else in the whole room as she yelled.

"Nigga is this the life you really want to live? You and Kevin suppose to meet me at college, remember? You and Kevin suppose to get our mommas out of the hood, remember? You and Kevin is all we have remember?"

Silence. Neither John nor Kev spoke a word. They knew exactly what Jazz was talking about. They had both talked to her on many occasions about their future, and had promised they would work hard at school, so they could attend college. They had made those promises to work towards a better life for their mother's and family, and Jazz believed in them.

John was so lost for words, as tears filled his eyes. He didn't know if it was a sign from God, telling him to stop while he was ahead, or if he was just having a guilty conscious. He sensed Kev wasn't feeling right either. All he could do was shake his head and look at the floor.

Mama took the bat next,

"John, I can't believe you! Didn't you and Kevin see what happened to Bernard and Van? I saw y'all join that nonsense! I done told y'all a thousand times, about the White man and his puppets. I can't believe y'all have fallin' for that nonsense."

Mama shook her head from side to side as she talked and tears rolled from her eyes onto her cheeks in rivers. Miss Goodman felt the same pain and put her palms to her face, and bent her head down towards her knees. They sat side by side on the couch sobbing. The hurt bound them together in unrelenting pain over the loss of Loco and Van, and now from their two babies joining the Crips.

John was unable to watch his mother cry, so he signaled for Donita and Meosha to go to his room. Jasmine looked at him and rolled her eyes. She asked a question about his decision to join the Crips, but John ignored her. The crying was really getting to him. He never experienced death at such close quarters, and wasn't accustomed to all the crying. He was ignorant to the fact that some of those grieving tears were for him. The extent of hurt and pain he was contributing to their lives, never entertained him.

Donita and Meosha headed towards the room, and John and Kev tried their best to ignore Jasmine's questions.

"Don't trip," John said, "I promise, I got this."

TERRY WROTEN

John tried to give her a hug, but she pushed him away.

"Nigga get off me! I don't want a hug from you. You rather be with them Crip niggaz out there, instead of in here with me and Momma."

Nothing John said could pacify Jasmine. She was trying to make him throw in his rags already, and he hadn't even been a Crip for an hour.

In John's room, he knew he had to explain the situation to Donita and Meosha. Kev was passive when it came to the True Blue, so he thought it was a waste of time to attempt to explain his decision. It annoyed John that Kev seemed to have a lack of conscious, so he decided that it was best he did all the talking.

"Ay, look this is how things gon' be..."

The Bloods had instantly started a war when Loco and Van were killed. That meant John and Kev had to *ride or die*, so John wasted no time in telling Donita the truth. He told her that he loved her, and that he didn't want to hurt anyone's feelings, but that he and Kev had made a choice to join the Crips and it would change their lives. He tried not to be harsh while explaining the situation, but he had to keep it real. He dwelled on the issue at hand and went on and on about it. He even told them, "Just because Kev and I are Crips now, don't mean we don't still love y'all."

It was hard for John to express his feelings, but the girls understood, and chose to ride with the two young Crips.

John had to make sure that Meosha and Donita were on their team. He wasn't proud of himself, but he played with their emotions making them choose between them and their families. They didn't need snakes, so it was important they were loyal. On this day, they all lost a part of their youth.

They talked until it was time for them to go, and when John opened his bedroom door they could all see Mama and Miss Good-

NATURAL BORN KILLAZ

Goodman still sitting on the couch sobbing. They avoided them, choosing the back door.

Outside, the block was congested with Crips and the homies were still hanging out: smoking, drinking, shooting dice, and just standing around as though it was the only thing in the world left to do. John held Donita's hand as they stepped out of the door and Kev followed lead with Me-Me. They were flaunting their girls. John smiled when Midnight spotted them, "Damn, lil cuzz, like that?" he asked.

He and Kev nodded.

Midnight turned towards Killa, who was leaning against a street lamp and indicating to the four of them, he lowered his voice and whispered, "You know, you gotta lace them on that part of the game."

John read Midnight's lips and knew exactly what he meant. Killa raised his eyebrows, "Yeah they know the game and I trust them lil' girls. Did you see them today, trying to help with the fight?"

What Killa and Midnight didn't realize was that Kev and John were aware of their conversation. This wasn't until John said, "Cuzz y'all not slick. That's already taken care of." Killa smiled. He knew John was good at reading lips. John had started to become interested at around five years old, and by the time he was eleven he considered himself a professional lip reader. He recalled sitting in front of his bedroom window watching Killa and Loco out front and wondering what they were talking about. He was so fascinated with his big brothers; he wanted to know everything they discussed.

"So where yall going?" asked Midnight.

Before John could answer, Crazoe and his crew came mobbing over to where they stood. John frowned and balled his fist; he was still heated from their earlier encounter. He heard Kev sigh and

and knew it was about to go down.

Killa immediately sensed the animosity and said, "Y'all can't be mad about what happened earlier. Y'all wanted to join this Crip thang, so ya'll have to accept what happened. Y'all gotta get over that or it will be a whole lot mo' jumpin'. This is what y'all chose to do, so deal with it!"

John looked at Killa, then at Kev, then at Crazoe. They all wanted to say something, but Midnight cut those thoughts off, "So aint y'all gon' walk y'all lil momma's home?"

John and Kev nodded.

"Wait a minute," Killa added. "Since y'all gon' have to learn how to get along, Crazoe, you and the young Westside homies walk with 'em."

John let out a deep breath, he hated Killa's decision. How in the hell was he and Kev suppose to walk with Donita and Me-Me with the dudes that jumped them? Luckily Midnight had his own version of unification, "Now Killa, let them boys have peace of mind with their girls. They don't need a crowd."

Killa nodded in agreement, "Y'all got ya'll burners?"

John and Kev lifted their shirts to expose their guns and walked off.

Later that night, the block was almost empty. A few Westside and Southside Crips were still hanging out, but other than the block was dry. The hood was known to house what niggas called the Category Gangstas and All Around Gangstas. The difference between the two was, the Category Gangstas were dudes from the hood but only joined the gang out of peer-pressure. They were the dudes who weren't going to kill a fly in a bar fight.

They were the pretty boys and the thieves. On the other hand, the All Around Gangstas were a different breed, they were the dudes who did everything that involved gangbangin'. They were

NATURAL BORN KILLAZ

the killers in the hood. They were considered superior because they were in the minority and the elite. John and Kev were instantly recruited as elite gangstas.

The All Around Gangstas from the West and South were the only Crips that stayed on the Eastside to help put in work. It had become their way of life, a life that was void of any normal humanity. After Killa had given instructions on their various missions, the All Around Gangstas signaled and formed a C with their index fingers and thumbs. Then they sped off.

John was amazed at the power his brother held over the gangstas. Killa was a professional hit man and his name spelled, *The Truth*. He planned to hit every Blood sect in Los Angeles. He planned his moves acquiring gloves and ski masks, and arranged stolen cars in the colors of red, white, black, and beige. By doing this he planned to catch the Bloods off guard. "The element of surprise is always the best art of war," Killa said. John liked the strategy.

Obeying Killa's instructions, John climbed into a white 1984 two door Regal along with Killa, Midnight, Kev, and Crazoe. The only thought in their minds were to hit the project Bloods. Kev, Crazoe, and John shared the back seat. It was Kev and John's first attempt at uniting with Crazoe. Midnight took the wheel as Killa joined him in the front of the car. From the passenger seat, Killa inspected everybody's guns. John and Kev handed over their .22s, and Killa checked the clips and the springs while showing them how to work the small killing machines. Crazoe had two .357s and an Uzi.

John wondered why Crazoe had three guns. Killa answered his thoughts by saying, "Crazoe you got thirty three rounds in the clip of the Uzi, use the five-sevens only for back up, and don't do anything stupid."

"Of course," John thought. " No wonder Crazoe got three burners. He gotta have back up John mentally checked himself for being so stupid. At that moment, he almost asked Killa for another, but thinking about it he remained content with what he had. It was the first time in the fields for him, and as the atmosphere grew more dense, he settled back and anticipated his night on the prowl. He remained silent.

The car of Crips entered the maze that was known as the Projects, and turned down the third block. Killa wanted to make his move as quick and lethal as possible. The Projects were dangerous; they were a death trap just waiting to happen. So they hit the first group of Bloods they came across.

The Bloods were gathered in a group, smoking, drinking, and shooting dice. Killa instructed his men to duck down as they drove pass. Midnight could not believe that not one of the Bloods acknowledged the car as they drove pass, "We got 'em," he said.

As Midnight parked the car on the nearest corner, Killa instructed the rest of the Crips on the plan. They were to use the cars parked on the block as camouflage, and make their way, unnoticed toward the Bloods. Then, John and Kev were to run towards them emptying their clips. When everybody was laid down, they were to run back to the car. Meanwhile, Crazoe and Killa would clean everything up, making sure that no one survived. Midnight's responsibility would be to keep the car engine running.

John could hear his heart pounding in his head as he and Kev crept behind the cars. After what seemed like an eternity, they were only inches away from the Bloods. It was then that one of them finally looked up from the dice game, but Kev was on him. He tried to yel,l "watch out", but Kev was already empting his clip and yelling, "Fuck slobs!"

His .22 barked. Pop, pop, pop, pop, pop, pop!

John remained silent as he put his .22 into the forehead of one of the Bloods who he caught slippin' on to his knees with the dice still

NATURAL BORN KILLAZ

in his hands.

Pop, pop, pop!

His .22 barked with vengeance as three slugs entered his first victim's head. Quickly turning, he aimed toward another Blood and emptied three slugs into his torso. Adrenaline still pumping, he and Kev ran back to the car.

Looking over their shoulders as they ran, John and Kev were reminded why Crazoe was given his name. He was defiantly crazy! John was also now arware of why Killa had told him not to do anything stupid. Crazoe yelled as he killed, "Nigga, this Crip! Nigga, Crip here!" Crazoe became louder as he continued to shoot.

Killa had two AKs in his hands; he looked like Rambo with both weapons. He didn't attempt to shoot; he was there to make sure everything went along as planned. After Crazoe had laid everything down with his Uzi, they waited a few seconds surveying the carnage, and then they jogged back to the car. Killing season had officially started.

CHAPTER 10
BRAZY B

It was commonly known that whatever you did on the Eastside someone would either know or find out. Word had a habit of spreading like wild fire, so it didn't take long before Brazy B received knowledge about John's new disposition as a Crip and a killer.

"Check!" he yelled as he and OG Red Flag sat contemplating their next move over a game of chess. They relaxed in Red Flag's guest room. He had a mansion in Rancho Cucamonga, and with a fire burning in the fire place and a fifth of Bacard on deck, the atmosphere was warm and drowsy. Since it was Scottie that had started the war, causing them to lose from all angles, they needed to strategize. With sixteen causalities on their side, money was being lost. Their drug trades were dropping, and at the moment funerals and strategizing had become top priorities.

Nevertheless, after knocking down two main figures with one stone within the Crip community, Brazy figured Killa and the Crips would stop. But Brazy was wrong because they hit with a vengeance ten times harder. Red Flag studied the board after being checked. He said, "Knight takes Queen out of check."

"Damn, I didn't see that," Brazy hissed.

"Brazy, I told you that this game is about strategy," answered Red Flag. "This is a game of life. When you strategize you got to play both sides of the board. You got to worry about what the next move might bring. A smart player stays three to five steps ahead to win the game."

Brazy half listened while he played the game; everything Red Flag said went in one ear and out the other. Surveying the board he said, "Bishop takes Knight! Check with my Rook! I just thought I'd let you know I always stay ahead of the game. After all, you are playin' against Brazy-Muthafucka- B!"

Red Flag chuckled. He was a veteran at strategy. He knew Brazy B was a stubborn young dude, and the only way to set him straight was to show him. Smiling, he took much pleasure in saying, "Wrong! There are two reasons why I know that you're not on your game. First, Queen takes Rook checkmate! Second, just how you play this game is the same way you play your life. You think two steps ahead not three or five."

Brazy snapped. He knew exactly what Red Flag was referring too. His eyes blazed, "How in the hell can you say that, when I'm the one who's holdin' down the hood. Yo' old ass only come to the hood to collect money. May I inform you that this is not the seventies or the eighties, this is nineteen ninety four. War is war! We lose some! We win some! As long as we get up and keep fightin', we straight."

Red Flag shook his head in disbelief. Brazy seemed crazy to him. He had tunnel vision and Red Flag knew that he needed guidance, or their organization would have been wrecked. Red Flag sighed, "Brazy you are one hundred percent right, this is not the seventies or the eighties and that is why I stay the hell outta the way. I paid my dues and moved on after G-Rag was killed. I backed up because it's a new generation of Bloods and Crips, and y'all don't know the meaning of knuckling up. The only thing y'all know is how to pull a gun. Things have changed since Rag and me started this gangsta shit. Back then, it was all about money and protecting our neighborhood. Since he's gone everything has changed,

TERRY WROTEN

and that's the reason why I turned everything except the projects, over to you. Being our protégé, I had to give it to you. But if you can't maintain a steady head when things heat up, it won't be hard to find another young Lieutenant or soldier who wants the same status as you. Brazy you lettin' your emotions and physical actions outsmart you. Look atchu'! You got yo' arms crossed because you don't like what I am telling you. Whachu gon' do shoot me because I'm tryna open yo' eyes to a bigger picture?"

Brazy was frustrated. He knew all along that Red Flag hadn't asked him to drive all the way to Rancho Cucamonga just to play chess. What he hadn't known was that Red Flag was going to criticize his gangsta. Brazy thought that he was doing everything a real gansta in the nineties was suppose to do.

He looked at Red Flag and said, "Blood, you didn't have to come at me like that. I know yo' status and you know mines. I respect yo' gangsta a little too much to pull a gun on you! So it's obvious that you aint respectin' me. Blood, er'thing I do is for the cause. I stay three steps ahead of the game and I'll never go against you. Keepin' it gansta, I don't know what you're seein' that I ain't. Honestly, it was the little cat that just learned how to stop pissin' in his bed that started this shit. If he wasn't yo' captain, I woulda killed him already..."

Red Flag cut Brazy off. "See that's what I'm seein' and you're not! You're too quick to jump and pull a trigger or go to war. Little Scottie dug his own grave. That's already been established. But staying three steps ahead is the way to plan. In the projects, everybody knows that Scottie is the reason why we lost sixteen homies in one night. Like I told you, when you and Sandra killed those two Crips, you gotta think three steps ahead of the game. But you didn't! If you were, then you woulda set up a curfew for all the homies and a lot of lives would have been saved..."

NATURAL BORN KILLAZ

Brazy snapped again, this time he demonstrated his anger by knocking the chess pieces off of the board.

"Blood, whachu tryna say?" Brazy was hot. "If you tryna say I'm the reason for the homies gettin' killed, you can suck my dick! Blood, I don't gotta sit here and listen to this bullshit!"

Red Flag stayed cool. He knew Brazy didn't cause the war. He only wanted him to realize he was the leader of the gang and had to prevent certain things from happening if he could. "See look at yourself Brazy, you've proven my theory right. Now, be to honest, you could sit here and listen to an Original Gangsta and learn this knowledge I'm tryna spit, or you could walk out of this house a stupid jail bound nigga. You must realize these Crips have always out numbered us, and that's a double edged sword for them and us.

The good thing for us is, the smaller the better. We can keep control and order within our turf and make sure all the homies are making money. On the other hand, the Crips out number us and that's deadly, especially knowing the real deal of our equations. We're all fighting for territory. The more we expand the better it is for us. It's all over the struggle for money, power, respect, and territory. Since we are the minority in this struggle, we must use strategy and think ahead of the game."

Brazy nodded. But Red Flag still had not answered his question.

"I understand whachu saying, but you still didn't answer my question. Red Flag, are you tryna say I'm the reason the homies got and gettin' killed?"

Red Flag sat looking at the fire place and rubbing his chin. He was thinking over the best way to answer Brazy's question. He knew that Brazy had been flipping on and off throughout the whole conversation and didn't want things to go downhill. He needed to open Brazy's eyes to the facts. He took his time before answering. "Yes. To be honest, I believe and know that you are a better leader

TERRY WROTEN

than whachu' puttin' on. G-Rag and I taught you well and now you act like we never existed. This new generation of gangbangin' is wearing off on you. When you were comin' up, we had as many funerals in one year as y'all have in one week! So yes, I believe that you are responsible. But I'm also responsible, so don't start lettin' yo' emotions do the talkin'. We all need to tighten up our game."

"Okay," said Brazy. "I respect yo' beliefs as an OG, but I believe you coulda put it in a different way. I also believe yo' puppet is responsible, but I'm all ears."

Red Flag knew that Brazy was defensive. It was important that the war was stopped and just as important that Brazy understood why. Too many young Black men were dying. There was an increase of violent deaths and with casualties on the rise, the government were implicating new laws to try and stop gang violence.

"Brazy, I wantchu to understand, I'm only gettin' at you this way because our situation. Young Blood, we are against all odds. Our game is so loose; it's like a car without a wheel alignment. And another point; that girl Sandra is runnin' her mouth about the set up, and that's not good..."

"What?" Brazy snapped.

"It's true. Sandra told Shante, and you know my wife got the biggest mouth ever. You know how niggaz and bitches pillow talk. So this means we have to tighten up in certain areas before we all end up in jail. It's important to take some time out to regroup."

"Imma kill that bitch, Blood," Brazy snarled.

"Naw! Naw! Don't you even think about touchin' that girl. Whatchu do is set her straight, but don't touch her, because I already checked her and told her I was gon' get at you about her runnin' her mouth."

Brazy's face grew dark as thunder, "Damn you, Flag! You are forty three and you know you shouldn't have told her shit. But you

NATURAL BORN KILLAZ

told her shit. But you know what? I don't even care because I got somethin' fo' her ass! And I want you to tell me what you fussin' about? What's the big deal with this shit on the streets? War is war."

    Red Flag took a sip of Bacardi, "Brazy we aint fit to stay at war with the Crips. We need to throw in our rags and call a peace treaty. I know it sounds like a cowardly move, but it's all about strategy. We need to regroup and lace our soldiers better than what we have been doing. We've lost sixteen homies and we are running out of money fast. We need a treaty for our own good, and don't worry about Scottie; he's as dead as a door-knob. We'll use him until time permits."

CHAPTER 11

May 30th and the duration of 1994

Faithful Star was the biggest church in the hood which seated 4000 people. It was where Crips from every block, city, and state came to pay their respects to Loco and Crip Van. Mama and Miss Goodman decided to have their son's funerals together and bury their bodies side by side. The sea of massed blue that flocked to their funerals bought over 3000 Crips alone, and many stayed outside to guard the church.

Killa let Killa Black and Killa Kev borrow his Lexus for the funeral, and Donita and Me-Me decided to ride with them for support. They all wore blue and white, Killa Black and Killa Kev wore matching blue Armani suits with white gators, while Donita and Me-Me dressed in blue DKNY skirts, white tops, and white pumps.

Viewing the bodies was the hardest thing that Killa Black have ever experienced. Looking at his brother firmly fixed in a casket ripped his heart right open. He instantly broke down and could hear Kev's broken sobs behind him. Donita and Me-Me tried to put on a brave face, but their boyfriends's pain was also theirs.

After the service and burial the crowd journeyed back to Mama's house for the repast. Killa Black and Killa Kev hung around outside with the homies, while Donita and Me Me stayed inside helping Jazz and Momma with the food. Crazoe and the homies from the Westside were hanging out with all of the young Eastside Crips, and over a short period of time the two cliques had grown closer

NATURAL BORN KILLAZ

to each other. After a few days of putting in work together, Killa Black and Killa Kev came to the conclusion that Crazoe and Midget were to be the Lieutenants on the Westside, and they were to be the lieutenants on the East. After witnessing Crazoe live up to his name in the projects, they knew he was a true gangsta. And after Crazoe seen them put in work, he knew they were ridas. In addition, even though Kev's attack on Midget was vicious, they knew Midget was down. Midget couldn't fight, but he never turned down a challenge, so they respected his gangsta.

The Crips stood outside Mama's house hanging on the sidewalk about twenty deep and the only person over the age of eighteen was Midnight. John's crew wore airbrushed shirts that read *R.I.P Loco and CripVan*. The whole crew was gangbanged out in gang attire, but Popa out did everyone. He had a blue rag over his head like Tupac and another rag covering his mouth and nose cowboy style. The only part visible was his big curious eyes. Popa joined the gang two days after Killa Black and Killa Kev. Miss Goodman was devastated about him joining. Popa was her baby and only ten years old. She felt vulnerable being a single mother; the streets were like a monster that gobbled up all her kids. Even though Popa was only ten, his gun read .32 and he gangbanged as if he was a man of twenty.

"Ay, cuzz, lets go pop some slobs," he said with a snide grin while aiming his .32.

Killa Black and Killa Kev exchanged glances, all the homies were looking at each other as if to say, "What a good idea" but they all shook that thought off.

"Naw," Kev said, "Popa you too young to go put in work."

Popa looked at his brother and the rest of whole crew wanting to say something slick, but Midnight intervened, "Naw little cuzz. Don't worry about the Bloods. They don't want any problems."

TERRY WROTEN

Popa shook his head in disbelief, "Damn them niggaz some bitches."

The Bloods declared a peace treaty and cease-fire after losing 16 members in one night. They had thrown in their flags. The Crips didn't mind the cease-fire, they had won the war 16 to 3. They lost Loco, Van, and Charlie, but the Bloods had lost 5 in the projects, 3 from Brazy B's side, and 8 on the Westside. After they had begged for mercy, Killa and Midnight declared a peace treaty and the fire ceased.

~~~~~

Activating the peace treaty had turned John and Kev's lives back to normal. After missing school for three weeks, he and Kev returned. It took a lot of extra studying for them to catch up, but with the help of Donita and Me-Me, they earned enough credits to receive passing grades. It was good to slip back into their old ways of hanging with each other during lunch and nutrition. Donita and John played their normal *I love you* games, like rubbing their feet together under the table. Miss Phillips was glad to see John and gave him a tight motherly hug, "Welcome back! I'm sorry to hear about your brother."

John forced a smile, "Oh thanks. But don't trip, he's gone but never forgotten." Miss Phillips was his favorite teacher.

At school, a few changes had taken place. Everyone who had hung around John's crew joined the Crips, and those who did not still wore blue and used the word "cuzz." A new change emerged and if you were an outsider, you would have thought that the school colors were blue and gray instead of gold and purple. The situation took a turn for the worst when Miss Philips and the rest of the teachers learned of John and Kev's gang names. They were called to Mr. Rudy's office and he demanded to know how they got their street names. To the two emerging generals in the Crip community, it was none of his business of how they got their names.

Kev took it upon himself to put Mr. Rudy in his place, "Mr. Rudy, whatever we call ourselves in the streets is our business, just like whatever you call yourself at home is yo' business. So long as we take care of our school business, don't worry about us or our crew. A'ight?"

It was an understatement to say Mr. Rudy was stunned by Kev's boldness. He didn't know what to say. John looked at his beet red face and knew Kev had spooked him. Mr. Rudy was a smart man. He knew who they were. He knew their brothers were reputable Crips, and after finding out their nicknames, he knew they were reputable too.

Nonetheless, the two Crips decided to bow to authority of the school; during school hours, they used the titles of KB and KK. Outside of school they used the full names of Killa Black and Killa Kev. The after school hangouts remained at Jack-in-the-Crack, Miss Goodman, and Mama's house. Even Papa had kids at his elementary school claiming Crip. It was like a domino effect, John and Kev stopped claming and joined the Crips, then Popa's crew started claiming. This was a tradition in the Blood and Crip community. Bloods and Crips were being bred by the day, this was an evolution that was not good at all.

On weekends, John was busy with his own drug operations. Killa supplied him with crack and weed. He stopped serving hand to hand to supply his crew. The crew had three spots that Popa, Big Head, and Lil' Loco were in charge of. They worked each spot as if they were pros, and were earning so much money they hated to leave. Sometimes, John and Kev worked on the weekends to give them a break, and Donita and Me-Me would join them.

TERRY WROTEN

Money was coming so fast off the sale of crack, John and Kev decided to let Money Mike handle the selling of weed. Mike was so business orientated, he immediately formed a crew who sold weed out of an apartment across the street from Carver. The weed rolled and everyone who worked for Mike benefited from the profits.

On the Westside, Crazoe and Midget were also running weed and Midnight supplied them. Their empire was larger than the Eastside Crips. Anytime Killa, Killa Black, or Killa Kev needed assistance they were there for them. Business moved at an incredible rate and money was flowing. The LAPD hated the fact there was no way they could stop the flow. Detectives Gilmore and Gilbert framed homies all over trying to find an inside informant. The first person in John's crew to be hit was Big Head. He was released to the custody of his parents after two weeks of being locked up in Central Juvenile Hall.

When he was released, he was treated like the man of the month. He was the first to be incarcerated, so the crew celebrated his homecoming. It was a triple celebration, they had to celebrate the accomplishments of the drug sales, Donita's 14th birthday, and his release. The venue they chose was "World On Wheels Skating Rink". The rink was the spot to be at on weekends, it was considered the number one spot to hang out.

John and his crew arrived at the rink in brand new cars, courtesy of the drug trade. He and Killa Kev bought identical '94 Caprices. The whole crew had new cars, and was killing the streets with them. Well, that's what they thought until Crazoe and Midget pulled into the parking lot in their Chevy Impalas on chrome 13-inch Daytons with grey leather interiors to match their Georgetown blue and gray color paint.

Popa couldn't drive. Shit, at this time he couldn't even see over the steering wheel, so he rode with Killa Kev and Me-Me. Donita

NATURAL BORN KILLAZ

rolled with John. Crazoe bought his girlfriend Tameka, who was super ghetto with a capital 'G' and five months pregnant, and his brother Lil' Crazoe. All the other homies rode solo hoping to catch a girl or two. Around this time, John's whole crew combine was worth about a quarter of a million dollars in cash and assets. To make it even more ridiculus they were only teenagers, ages 14 and 15. The money was usually wasted on material things, so nothing positive came out of it.

After they parked, everyone in line waiting to enter the rink turned and stared. Most attention came from the adults who were stunned to see these young kids hop out of brand new cars adorned with gold rope chains, new Chuck Taylors, and blue rags. It was obvious to them that none of these young thugs were over the age of eighteen. However, they didn't say a word, just smiled and nodded. They knew these kids were Crips.

Inside the rink, Donita was surprised when she received her birthday presents; a pair of pink Chucks converted into skates from John and a gold rope chain from Kev and Meosha. John was also surprised when Kev handed him a pair of blue Chucks converted into skates. He and Donita said, "Thanks" in unison.

Kev nodded, "Cuzz, that aint nothin'. Y'all know how we do it. Let's get our clown on."

Hitting the skate rink floor was battle time as usual, especially for John and Kev. They were considered the best skaters at Carver. All eyes had been on Crazoe and Midget until they hit the floor. Kev raised his voice over the music, "Y'all Westside niggaz can't fuck with us Eastside niggaz on skates."

Hearing Killa Kev, Midget screwed up his face. He was one of the best skaters on the Westside and had his every move down pack. He knew Killa Black and Killa Kev could fight, but when it came to skating they couldn't mess with him or Crazoe.

TERRY WROTEN

He yelled, "Putcha money where yo' mouth at."

Midget resembled Gary Coleman so John taughted, "Whachu talkin"bout Willis?"

John was cracking a joke, but Crazoe was serious. He said, "Two hundred."

Kev countered, "Three," while moving his feet in a backwards motion.

"Four," spat Crazoe.

John got tired of all the talking, "Fuck it, five!"

"Bet!" Crazoe and Midget blurted.

John had a gut feeling that Crazoe and Midget were going to be a match, so he only agreed on the terms that the DJ and the audience were to be the judges. When everyone agreed, they walked to the DJ's booth, handed him $1000 combined and asked him to play "Big Poppa", by Notorious B.I.G. At the time, Notorious wasn't getting much radio play on the West Coast, but he was gaining a lot of recognition with his song "Big Poppa". Everyone on the West Coast seemed to be into Death Row. Snoop Dogg and Dre were played in just about every black household. However,'"Big Popp'" was John's main jam and it was the song he chose.

As the DJ announced the battle over the loud speaker, he asked everyone to clear the floor. Donita yelled, "Y'all smash 'em baby."

John and Kev nodded.

"I love it when you call me Big Pop-pa," the music started playing, as Crazoe and Midget took to the floor first. They clowned and ripped the floor up, but when it was time for John and Kev to perform they did their staged battle routine; Kev hit the floor first and clowned by himself, then John came gliding in. They held hands skating backwards then Kev purposely fell so as John could leap over him and start clowning by himself. John would skate a lap, then Kev hopped up and they continued to clown until the end of

NATURAL BORN KILLAZ

the song, where in unison they hit a back flip to win.

The crowd went crazy when they landed the flips.

After the DJ announced them the winners, John and Kev split the money. When *"couples only"* was announced over the loud speakers John grabbed Donita, and the rest of the crew grabbed partners. Midget grabbed himself a fine red bone girl with green eyes. John smiled seeing Big Head and Lil Loco in the corner pocket with two butt naked high school girls. Even Papa had a girl for the night and they were having fun.

John and Kev were having it their way just like *Burger King*, because they finally got Meosha and Donita to agree on letting them be their first. Crazoe and Tamika stopped skating because she was tired and her back was hurting. Midget was tongue kissing the sister he just met. Money Mike and the rest of his crew were mingling and having fun. It was a trip when the DJ announced, "Would the birthday girl Donita and her future husband Killa Black please stay on the floor?"

Donita and John stopped skating and looked toward the DJ booth. They laughed at Kev and Meosha's smiling faces and at Kev throwing up the C.

"This song is for Killa Black and Donita," the DJ announced. "Happy birthday Donita, from Kev, Meosha, and the rest of the crew."

'Twelve Play' by R. Kelly started playing. John held Donita's waist as he towered over her small frame, kissing and licking her neck. Looking up at him she whispered, "John, I love you."

John damn near fell over. He was in love just as much as Donita. He looked into her eyes saying, "I love you more." He then planted a kiss on her cheek. Their moment to shine on the skating rink floor was over when the DJ told everyone they could join the birthday girl and her husband. Kev had paid $50 to get them five minutes on the floor and that was cool!

After they finished skating, Donita and John walked over to the snack shop. He bought two ice lemonades and a pack of *Sour Powers*. Instead of waiting for the DJ to announce "*glow sticks only,*" he bought four blue ones.

John just made the purchase when the announcement came on. It was at that moment that he remembered Big Head. It was suppose to be his welcome home celebration, and he hadn't even taken anytime away from Donita to holla at him. He knew Killa had given him a new car. He had also received $3000 from John and Kev. Money Mike and Lil' Loco bought him new gear, but John still felt bad ignoring him because he was his boy and a good worker.

After looking for Big Head and looking toward the corner pocket, John spotted him looking like a man who did not want to be bothered. He knew "get out of jail pussy" was the best pussy, so he kept going about his business with Donita.

"*411*" by Mary J. Blige began to play when John tossed Kev and Meosha their glow sticks. They hit the floor and the girls tried to make their pink Chucks look like a million bucks, but the boys' blue Chucks and blue glow sticks were killing the game. Everyone groaned when the DJ announced the rink would be closing in two minutes. They were all having fun but it was time to leave, so they rallied up the troops. Popa was the only one missing, but Kev knew exactly where he was at, "Popa come on!" he yelled.

Papa came running out of the corner pocket pulling up his pants, "Damn, I was gettin' some pussy," he snarled. "Why you hatin'?"

Kev snapped, "Cuzz, shut up and bring yo' ass on! You was only humpin'."

"So what!" Papa replied, "I was getting some."

NATURAL BORN KILLAZ

"Man whatever. Lets go!" Kev spat playfully slapping Popa in the back of the head.

At the time, Kev was working on his attitude so he appeared to have characteristics of a person who had been dianosed as Bi-polar. To the crew, he was interesting to watch, snapping one minute then calming down next. He and Meosha had guidelines for each other: he was working on his temper and she was working on her ghetto ways. They left the skate rink but when they reached the cars Kev could not help himself from bragging at the top of his voice about the money they'd won. He went on and on about how the Eastside boys dominated everything. Kev was known to speak his mind and so was Crazoe.

"Alright, cuzz!" Crazoe blurted. "Y'all won. Do you wanna cookie or somethin'? That five hundred y'all won, we make in an hour. That's change. Plus, Midget decided to donate a little money to our fellow broke Eastside homies."

Midget looked up and smiled, "Crazoe, dontchu feel real good? Sharin' is carin'. Like they say what goes around comes around. We gave five, we get ten."

John didn't like the tag team game Crazoe and Midget started to play he said, "Shit, that's five free hundred. I'm blessed to have homies that care."

"Yeah that's good lookin'." Kev couldn't contain himself from adding in his two cent. "Anyway, Black and I gotta get back to the hood. We got some extra business to handle. If y'all know what I mean?"

It was hard not to know what Kev meant as he hinted towards Moesha and Donita by moving his head from side to side and pointing.

TERRY WROTEN

~~~~~~

It was around six in the mornin when they made it back to the spot. Killa Black sent Popa and the rest of the homies home. He and Kev needed to take their relationships with Donita and Me-Me to the next level. He thought about everything Killa told him about sex and what he heard from other dudes on the block. He took it nice and slow, rugged and hard, mean and fast. He experienced his first orgasm and instantly realized why the female species are so powerful. He was elated about getting his first piece of pussy.

CHAPTER 12

KILLA

May 1995

Summer of 1995 was fast approaching and Killa knew the hood was going to be hot. The LAPD and Governor Pete Wilson were putting their summer time sweep together and Killa knew the best way to beat the draft was to keep the homies out of the red zone. At the time, the red zone was the hood and anything in the ghetto, so Killa threw barbeques at his house in Marina Del Rey. The Crips were not aware of his strategy. John wondered why he began to allow the homies to hang at his residence. Later on in life John would learn why Killa was so successful at being a leader and the reasons why he was not.

Killa stood outside his house washing his drop-top '63 Impala, while the batteries to his hydraulic system charged. He was getting ready for later that evening. It was Sunday so Crenshaw Boulevard was the place to be. Crenshaw on Sundays meant a block party, especially when summer time was approaching. On Sundays, it was familiar to see Crips, Bloods, hustlers, pimps, players, professional athletes, actors, ghetto queens, snakes, gold diggers, and women in three piece suits. Every one hit the strip to floss and flaunt their rags to riches.

John called from Mama's house to see what was on Killa's agenda and Ebony answered the phone, so he left a message for Killa. Ebony walked outside and delivered I,. "Baby, John just called and said him and the crew are on their way. Al Dog, also called and said him

NATURAL BORN KILLAZ

and Gangsta MC will meet you on the boulevard around ten before midnight."

Al Dog and Gangsta MC were from the Southside. They were originally Eastside Crips, but since their hood was located in southeast Los Angeles, they were Southside Crips. Al Dog was the General on that side of town and known as a cold killer. Gangsta MC was his roll dawg but was not a Crip, nevertheless he was a cold triggerman, and gangsta in his own right. Niggas on the streets reffered to him as the *"'gangsta and the gentleman,,* because even though he wasn't officially a Crip, every Crip in Los Angeles respected his gangsta.

Killa looked up from wiping his rims and asked, "Did Al Dog say if he was drivin' his Rida?" Killa was referring to Al Dogs lowrider. He knew Al Dog and MC had some of the hottest cars and wanted to know that he wasn't going to be riding alone. He had a gut feeling that MC was going to flaunt his '64 Impala, since it was the hottest car in South Central. Ebony replied, "No. Al Dog didn't say what car he was driving, but John said him and Donita are coming out here together and everybody's cars are full. Look like we gon' have a full house. Also, can I follow you in yo' Bentley when we hit the Shaw tanite?"

Killa frowned. He hated the fact that he had spent so much money on Ebony's BMW and Mercedes that she begged him for, but hardly ever drove. In fact, she drove his Lexus and Bentley more than he did. He was starting to believe he had bought her cars for nothing. Not only was he frowning from her question, he frowned at the thought of knowing her plot. He knew that she was asking for the Bentley so she could carpool with Donita, Meosha, and Tamika. He despised the whole thought, especially since he knew whom Donita and Me-Me belonged too. He was still uptight from John and Kev joining the gang, so he lost his temper. He cursed up a storm taking his frustrations out on her, but Ebony was his true other half and knew he was stressing over his two brothers.

Ebony let him curse until he grew tired, "Benjamin, I'm not stupid! You could blame and curse me all you want, but I know the real problem. The same problem has been bothering you for the last year. We both know everytime you talk to Mama and she tell you how John and Kevin are gettin' worse, you have a guilt trip. So don't take yo' problems out on me, especially if I didn't do nothing but ask to borrow yo' car."

Killa nodded. He was aware that he was flipping out on her for other reasons. The car issue was not that big. He felt bad and apologized, "Baby, I'm sorry. I'm just trippin' off Mama's speech from this morning. Why you think I came out here? I need peace of mind, so stop asking to borrow my car when you got two brand new ones."

Ebony knew she was becoming a pest about the car issue, so she decided to let Killa vent,

"Baby, I swear, I've never felt like this before. Something keeps tellin' me I am going to be the next one to die. I don't know where this feeling is comin' from, but what I do know is my bangin' days are over! I don't wanna get too deep into this conversation until later, so can you just go get er'thing ready for company?"

"Er'thing is already taken care of," said Ebony. I just gotta dress Benjamin and put the meat on the grill. And I take it, your response to my question is no, right?"

Killa shook his head, "You sho' know how to get what you want when it comes to me, huh? You know even if I wanted to say no, I couldn't. Well, at least, not to you."

Ebony cracked a one-sided smile and turned on her heels. She knew she had a good man.

When John pulled up to Killa's house with the rest of his crew and some Westside Crips, he immediately knew that Killa wasn't

NATURAL BORN KILLAZ

feeling the situation. He read his thoughts and just knew what he was thinking, "Damn! John, you are just like me. Now, I see what I've put Mama through." Killa's thoughts soon turned in the way of Killa Kev as he pulled up, parking right behind Killa's Impala.

"Big Killa Loc, what it is cuzz?" Kev greeted.

Killa looked at Kev and shook his head. Gangbangin' was something he preferred them not to do, but these young Crips were doing it hard. Even Popa was starting to make a name for himself in the streets.

Killa shrugged, "It is what it is..." He paused and didn't continue with the rest of the traditional Crip saying. This is led John believe his assumption that Killa was not feeling the situation was true.

He didn't finish the saying but Papa did by saying, "Cuzz, it is what it is, this Crip shit is the biz."

When all the homies arrived at the house, it was packed. John looked at Killa as he stood, holding the railing of his upstairs balcony looking down at everyone. Ebony and Donita were at the grill watching John and gossiping between themselves. Tameka was breast-feeding her and Crazoe's newborn, and John and the homies were in a circle. John stood a little way out of it looking up at his brother on the balcony. He watched Killa's every move until Midnight appeared, put his arm around Killa and asked, "What is it?" Midnight had sensed the same uncomfort in Killa as John had.

John tuned into their conversation.

"It's a long story," said Killa. "I'm stressed out."

Midnight nodded, "Talk to the old man. I'll talk back."

Killa let out a deep breath, "Remember that talk we had after Lefty died? When I told you, I would never be the same. Well, now, since Loco and Van is gone it's time for me to go too."

John's heart skipped a beat, he didn't understand what Killa meant by his statement and neither did Midnight.

TERRY WROTEN

"Oh shit! Killa, don't be talkin' about killin' yourself!"

Killa chuckled, "I've got too much to lose and two sons to raise. I ain't never talkin' about no suicide."

"So whachu' talkin' 'bout? Because you lost me!"

John was lost too, lost and puzzled, but he never lost focus on their conversation.

Killa shuffled as if to get more comfortable for his next words, "Midnight, I've been talkin' to my Cuban connection Sammy, and I've been thinkin' 'bout movin' out there. Man, I feel these White folks gon' be comin' to wreck shop any minute or imma end up dead and what make things worse, I got my baby brother out here killin' shit. Cuzz, I know this don't sound like the real me, but this gangbangin' shit is ain't for me no more. Cuzz, look at all these young dudes we got down there livin' this fucked up life, and it's fucked up because the next time we look up, the majority of those dudes are gon' be dead or in jail."

Midnight nodded in agreement. He knew Killa was coming from the heart and had no feelings for the street anymore. He clinched Killa's left shoulder with his left hand and fingertips, while moving his fingers in a massage type motion,

"Cuzz, I already know how you feel. You ain't the only person tired of this bullshit. I've been wantin' to turn my rags in, but it's somethin' in my heart that's pullin' and resistin'. Not only that, but my sister don't wanna quit her job at that school; and you know I aint goin' nowhere without her. But whatever you decide I'm gon' ride witchu'..."

As the conversation continued between Killa and Midnight, John put two and two together from Midnight's statement and what Miss Phillips had told him a year prior, and he concluded Midnight was the brother Miss Phillips referred to. As they talked Ebony interrupted them from the hot grill, "Baby, your food is done! Do you

NATURAL BORN KILLAZ

want me to bring two plates up there?"

Killa looked down and caught John ear hustling. John played it off and answered the question for his brother. "Hell naw! Make 'em come get in line like everybody else."

Killa chuckled, "Is that right?" He then looked at Ebony, "Baby, since we gotta come down there make sure John eat last."

Ebony shook her head in agreement, but Donita already had made John's plate. She smiled and said, "Sorry Killa my baby's plate is already made."

Killa and John smiled to each other as he walked down the stairs. It was a known fact that their gangsta divas were on the move. Donita and Meosha were becoming the sort of females only a gangsta could have, and with Ebony as their big sister and mentor, Killa Black and Killa Kev could not have wished for anything more.

~~~~~~

Later that night, they hit Crenshaw and it was off the hook. Jasmine came over to pick up the kids so she could babysit. This freed up Ebony and Tameka. They, along with Donita and Me-Me, carpooled in Killa's Bentley as he swerved and dipped ahead driving his Impala. Crenshaw, known as *The Shaw,* was the spot where all South Central's finest parked their cars along the street; often posing next to them. Every now and again, there was a battle between cars and car club, over who had the hottest ride. But the main focus was who had the most money, best dressed, and who stood out in the crowd. The Shaw had been off the hook since the 80's and so it remains to this day. Sisters hit the Shaw from all over; they come dressed in the finest fashion, checking out rides and displaying their values and assets.

As the Crip entourage slowly pulled up to The Shaw, Killa hit a switch and lifted his back bumpers off the ground. John watched from four cars behind. The whole hood knew how grimmy niggas on Crenshaw could be, so even before they left, Killa set up the route they were suppose to roll. It went as follows: Killa, Midnight, Ebony and the girls, Big Head, Little Loco, John, Kev, and then the rest of the homies.

While Killa performed his tricks, John spotted Al Dog, Gangsta MC, and the other Southside Crips. They were all leaning on MC's Impala. They smiled and threw up the 'C'. They already secured a couple parking spots for Ebony, Killa, and Midnight. The Shaw was crowded so the rest of the crew had to go in search of parking spots. While they were out searching for spots to park, Killa started to wonder what was taking them so long; especially John, Kev, and Crazoe. All the other homies had parked and made it to base.

Killa called Ebony over to him. He now was leaning on MC's hood while Ebony and the other divas stood in their own circle. The circle of divas were all armed and dangerous. They posed as bodyguards and this was convenient to the Crips because these girls were not targets for the LAPD.

"Ebony, I need you and the divas to hit the stripe and find John and 'em," said Killa.

Ebony turned on her heels, signaled to her self-proclaimed gang of gangsta divas, and nodded.

Killa watched as she and her crew strolled off. He silently cursed 'damn' to himself. Ebony's hourglass figure looked marvelous through her Fendi outfit. As Midnight and the others engaged in an in-depth conversation about the streets, Killa grabbed a bottle of Cristal and took a drink. He drifted off into his own thoughts ignoring Midnight and Al Dog's conversation. It was apparent that he was losing interest in the streets. Popping bottles of Cristal on The Shaw was a way of showing others you had plenty of money, but the hype did not worry Killa. His main concern was for John, and Mama's lecture,s which were eating him from the inside out.

NATURAL BORN KILLAZ

As he took swigs off the drink, Loco and Big Head came running into view. Killa's heart immediately dropped, he knew something was wrong,

"Cuzz, what's wrong with y'all?" Killa asked.

Loco was exhausted from running and it took a while for him to catch his breath, "Killa we are about to shut this down," he replied.

Killa was buzzed from the Cristal but was always prepared to handle business. His buzz seemed to vanish. Loco's and Big Head's breath came in short and hard bursts as they related the story of parking their cars when a contingent of Bloods rolled past.

Midnight who was now more than interested asked, "Where they at?"

Big Head waved his arms, "Around here somewhere."

Killa's stomach started to flutter, "Where the hell is John and Kevin?"

Big Head shrugged, "We thought they would be back here already. We spotted them doin' a U turn and Crazoe was right behind them."

Killa cursed, "Damn! I hope them niggaz didn't do anything stupid." He turned on his heels and the crew followed. He mobbed down The Shaw with an attitude that read: I'm the hardest nigga to walk these streets. All the hood rich niggas and ghetto superstars acknowledged him as he made his way through the various crowds and groups on the strip. As he walked, Loco said, "Cuzz there they go!" He pointed at John, Ebony, the girls, and the Bloods.

Killa quietly contemplated the scene as he waited for the traffic to slow down. John was across the street talking to Brazy B. Killa ordered Big Head and Midget to stand guard on their side of the street. As John caught sight of his brother, he knew that he had to be wondering what Brazy and he was talking about, while Crazoe, Kev, Ebony, and Tameka stood with their guns exposed. Donita and

TERRY WROTEN

Me-Me stood in-between the Bloods and them. It was an odd situation for Killa to fathom. Bay-Bay suddenly saw Killa and yelled, "Aww Blood! That's Killa!!"

The Bloods immediately reached for their guns. Their reaction almost triggered a shoot out.

Brazy yelled, "Hell naw! Blood, it aint even like that! Not with my lil' sister out here!"

Hearing Brazy speak his peace for his side, Killa did the same knowing that the cease-fire and peace treaty was still active, but he was puzzled at the scene in front of him. After both sides put the guns away, he made his way towards the crowd, "What's this all about?" He demanded when he made it over to Brazy B and John.

Brazy was stunned, surprised that he and Killa were standing face to face without trying to gun each other down. It was his dream to catch Killa slippin' and blow his head off, but he knew he had to stay three steps ahead of the game. He greeted Killa with a forced smile, "Benjamin 'my boy' Wilson Jr. aka O.G. Killa Loc. Man, how's these hectic streets treatin' you? It's been a long time since our friendship ended and you and Michael went one way and I the other. Them was the good old days. I was just tellin' John about 'em."

Killa looked at Brazy and shook his head. He knew exactly what Brazy was referring to. They were boys before the Red and Blue came into play, before they started sect trippin' on each other. He knew Brazy was still the same Daron Jackson that he had grown up with.

"Daron, you know the business with us and what it boils down to, you bang Red and I bang Blue; so what's the hold up with you and my lil' brother?"

Brazy sighed, he felt like a punk. He hated the fact he had to use his head in a gun battle.

NATURAL BORN KILLAZ

He knew he had to keep the peace and his word to Red Flag. There was a time and a place for gunplay and Crenshaw wasn't the place, especially with hundreds of witnesses watching.

"Damn, Ben, I hope I didn't strike a nerve talkin' to John. I mean, I can't stand the fact that a hoodrat told me that my lil' sista's boyfriend is a young commander for y'all. I couldn't believe it at first, but like I was just tellin' him, I still got mad love for yo' momma; so he's welcome to the pad anytime. I've been wantin' to tell you, *good lookin'* on the peace treaty and cease fire."

Brazy's words went in one ear and out the other. Killa wasn't a rookie. He knew the only reason the Bloods wanted a peace treaty was to regroup and strategize. The only reason he agreed to a peace treaty was because war meant casualties and less money. Killa smiled savoring his own thoughts and knew the peace treaty was benefiting both sides. After receiving word from Charlie about Diamond, he had decided using a little strategy himself. The name of his war tactic was called "divide and conquer', sort of like playing the role of a sucker to catch a bigger sucker.

He looked at Daron and with a half smile said, "Come on, you know like I know, we don't need no war over some bullshit; especially when we are makin' so much money. But to be honest, if I see that bitch you had with you the night my brother and Van got killed, imma kill her! That stupid bitch been runnin' her mouth like a faucet, so I know you had something to do with my lil' brother's murder. You need to fix your leak or imma do it for you."

Killa already knew his job was done. He knew Brazy was going to kill Diamond just from the thought of knowing she had ran her mouth.

After using his strategy of "divide and conquer" the Crips mobbed off. Red and blue lights were flashing in the distance.

TERRY WROTEN

It was a little after 12 o' clock and the LAPD were shutting The Shaw down.

CHAPTER 13

Summer of 1995

The alarm clock in the spot went off at eight in the morning, school was out and John and his crew were waiting for graduation. He and Kev were so exhausted from the long day they had the day before, they paid no attention to the alarm clock. It wasn't until Popa came banging on the door that they got themselves out of bed. Popa was causing such a commotion, Kev angrily hopped out of bed saying, "Hold the fuck up!"

As he opened the door, Popa and eight of his boys barged into the house, "Damn," Kev hissed, "Where y'all going?"

A snide grin spread across Popa's face, "We tryna go to the pool. It's the first day of summer vacation and we tryna get crackin' on some ho's."

Kev looked towards the ceiling rolling his eyes in disbelief, "No. Not now. I'm tired. We'll go tomorrow cause I'm bout to go back to sleep."

Popa and his boys had reached the age of eleven and twelve, and they determined not to miss the opening day of the pool. The pool was the same pool that held the 1984 Olympics, and it was the only place in the ghetto that attracted tourists. John decided to go along with them since he could not sleep with all the noise Popa was making. He hopped out of bed and walked into the living room, "A'ight cuzz, we'll go but who gon grab some ass for me?"

Popa's whole crew yelled, "We all are!"

NATURAL BORN KILLAZ

"What's the rules?" John asked.

Kev looked at John as if he was crazy. He wanted to go back to sleep, but he knew what goes around comes around. The pool was a traditional place the Crips hit in the summer, and when they were Popa's age they begged Killa, Loco, or Van to take them; so it was now their turn to take the younger generation. The young crew recited the only rule that Killa and his crew had made, "Whoever don't grab some ass can't move with us no more!"

After John persuaded Kev to come along, he called Donita and Meosha so that they could join them. Money Mike decided to roll with them as well. They arrived at the pool an hour later. Donita and Meosha took the situation as baby-sitting Popa and his crew, but John and Kev took it as looking out for the little homies. They enjoyed watching Popa's crew. They pointed to females and whoever grabbed her backside was rewarded with five bucks.

Money Mike pulled a high school girl that day and they enjoyed themselves. Things became hectic when Donita and Me-Me pushed John and Kev into the water. They retaliated with Popa and his crew joining in. They dunked the girls nonstop until Donita begged for mercy. The pool was so off the hook that day, it was added to their summer activities. That whole summer was spent having fun and it seemed to go so fast. John could not believe it when it came time to go back to school. Graduation was perfect as John walked the stage at Trade Tech Community College with his head held high. Mama cried when he received his Junior High Shcool Diploma.

With all the illegal out of school activities he was getting into, she doubted if he or his crew would walk across that stage. Even though they were rebellious and caught up on the streets, Mama never gave up on them. She cried as they, even Donita and Meosha, received their diplomas.

TERRY WROTEN

After the ceremony, John looked over at Miss Phillips and she was crying too. She indicated for him to join her, and he met her at the back of the auditorium,

"John, I'm so proud of you. I can't even explain how much I am going to miss you. But, anyway, I called you over because I want a hug and I want you to meet somebody."

John gave Miss Phillips a hug while Mama, Miss Goodman, and Miss Jackson stood a few feet away taking pictures. As they hugged, John felt Miss Phillips signaling for someone behind him. After breaking from the embrace, he was stunned. Killa and Midnight were behind him and both were wearing Armani suits. He never saw them sport a three piece with a tie, not even at Loco and Van's funeral. Miss Phillips smiled, "John, I want you to meet my brother Phil."

He mumbled, "Damn" while shaking his head and placing his palms on his cheeks. It was a small world after all.

"See I told you" Miss Philliphs said, "You thought I was playing when I told you, huh? I told you don't think you're the only one with a little hood or self-destruction in your blood. Just let me tell you something else in front of your two role models."

Miss Phillips lowered her voice to a whisper, "I was once a Crip! I did all the destruction a Black woman could do for what y'all call the hood. But I saw that I was heading down the wrong path, so I turned myself right around and went to college, got my PHD, now I'm teaching to help young brothers like you. John you can follow my footsteps; we don't need gangs of Red and Blue. We need gangs of Blackness and unity –"

Miss Phillips went on one of her brotherhood speeches and John was elated when Mama interrupted. Mama was getting a lot of use out of her camera that day; she wanted photos of Miss Phillips and

NATURAL BORN KILLAZ

John and more of John and his crew. John found it interesting to look at Midnight and Miss Phillips; the only way you could tell that, they were brother and sister was by their facial structures. Other than that, they looked nothing alike.

Graduation proved to be another turning point in John's life. After that day, Miss Phillips stopped working at Carver and was promoted to principal at a continuation school on the Westside. John moved on to high school. He was sent to Jefferson High, which was located on the border of the Crips and Bloods territory, but it sat on Blood territory.

On the first day of school, John and Kev met at Mama's house and from there they went to pick up Loco and Big Head. As soon as they arrived at the student parking lot, they knew there were going to be problems. They could almost feel the hate coming from the Bloods and their associates, but that didn't stop the young Crips from putting on their blue belts, blue rags, blue chucks, blue fat laces, and blue Dickies as they hopped out of the car. Money Mike pulled up right behind them with three homies, all wearing blue. This was the first day of school, and the Crips intended on making a lasting impression. They knew that they had to set an example as quickly as possible. They made a grand entrance with John leading the pack. They mobbed hard, like some kind of mafia figures and the Bloods, jocks, cheerleaders, nerds, and teachers had no doubts that they were Crips.

The bell for first period rang and they separated and went to class. Somehow, John and Kev ended up in the same subject classes. John wondered if Miss Phillips had pulled some strings for them. He worried about Donita and Meosha too. He had said it was okay for Donita to borrow his car since he and Kev were carpooling, and he hadn't seen them that morning. His worries were short-lived when Mr. Davenport, their first period teacher, called

TERRY WROTEN

"Donita Jackson and Meosha Thomas" for roll call. It was at that very moment they came swishing into class.

Kev look at Meosha and whispered, "Damn, what took y'all so long?"

She sighed, "None of yo' business."

John cracked a one-sided smile and Kev responded with a look that read, "Is that right?"

Exchanging schedules, they noticed that they all shared the same classes. John wasn't sure if Miss Phillips had some influence over the fact or if it was just good luck, but he did know that high school was starting off on the right track. During nutrition, they met up with all the other Crips and mobbed to the cafeteria, it was a popular meeting place during nutrition and lunch. They were the center of attention that first day. Everyone's head turned, word spread that Killa Black, Killa Kev, and the Crips had checked in. Hearts dropped when they entered. People knew that there was bound to be problems, especially Bool Aide and his crew. Their organization had heard that John and Kev were not only fighters, but gunners and Lieutenants too.

At the time, John was still learning how fast word could spread on the Eastside. Bool Aid started to approach him. He knew he didn't want any problems, that was apparent from the night they'd bumped heads on Crenshaw, when Bool Aide attempted to shake his hand.

John looked at Donita and the crew and told them, "Wait here."

At the back of the cafeteria, he looked Bool Aid in the eyes and said, "What's crackin'? What's the business?"

John didn't want to come off too hardcore and he didn't want to sound too soft. He only wanted to see if they were going to have to rock the place to set an example, or if they were going to leave *their beef on the streets.*

NATURAL BORN KILLAZ

"Look. Check it out, Black," Bool Aide replied, "I know you and Kevin are runnin' the Crips. It's all over the Eastside how y'all got y'all names. Dawg, to keep it 'G' my boys and me aren't trippin', if y all aint trippin'. We can *leave the beef on the streets* and go our own way durin' school. Nahmean?"

John poked his chest out and arched his brow, "So whatcha'll wanna do, knuckle up after school?"

Bool Aide looked a little concerned, "Naw! Naw!" he said, "It aint even like that. All I'm sayin' is we keep the peace, y'all keep y'all, and we leave it at that."

In John's head, his mission was complete. He wanted Bool Aid to bow down, and that's exactly what he did. At the time, he felt like the bigger man, but truth be told Bool Aide was. He was so naive he never asked himself, "why self destruct when you're in a position to better yourself"?

John walked back to where Kev and the crew had marked their new territory, and Kev did not hesitate to ask, "what the Bloods were talking about?"

"They talkin' 'bout that peace treaty shit," John informed. He knew Kev stayed on the prowl for trouble, so he tried to relate what Bool Aid said in simplistic te so he agreed letting Big Head be their gunman. rms.

Kev flipped, "Damn, cuzz! So you sayin' they don't wanna knuckle up either?"

"Naw," John replied.

Big Head looked disappointed.,"Damn, cuzz, I thought I was gon have to lay somethin' down today!"

Big Head was the only one in the crew with a gun. The rest of the Crips had decided not to carry pistols during school hours, but Big Head had a motto, *Never leave home without one.* John knew out of the whole crew Big Head was the one with the least fighting skills, so he agreed letting Big Head be their gunman.

The crew went on and on about the Bloods. Kev was the worst and kept instigating the situation, "Damn, cuzz, Popa got mo' heart than these slob-ass niggaz. On Crip, if any of these dudes look at me, it's goin' down. I can't believe we gon sit here without gettin' off in their ass. This shit make me feel like a punk or somethin'."

John had to calm Kev. He felt less than a man, the enemy were sitting less that a hundred feet away and that was a no-no to Killa Kev, "Damn, Kev, you know Killa already told us if these niggaz aint trippin', don't worry 'bout 'em. Just get our education and do us."

Kev gradually relaxed, knowing the enemies would be taken care of eventually. The rest of that first day in high school was good. Jocks and cheerleaders were fascinated by how the Crips represented themselves. The Crips received invitations to house parties, pool parties, football games, and all the other normal high school activities.

As months passed going to school, hustling ,and spending time with Kev, Donita, and Me Me became John's daily routine. They were all receiving passing grades and their relationships were above and beyond their expectations. Donita and Meosha had evolved from being Crip haters to Crip lovers. They were learning the game on a daily basis and they started working their own spots with Ebony. With the girls doing their own thing, business was moving fast and the Crips were expanding. They went from 3 crack houses to 8, from 1 weed apartment to 4 and, opened up an additional 3 houses.

Money was coming so fast; these kids contemplated dropping out of school. However, Killa was aware of their scheme and made sure that they promised to continue to receive passing grades. He didn't want them to make the same mistakes as he had and told them, even though he was aGgeneral, his empire was vulnerable and he didn't have an education to fall back on, "Ya'll" he said,

NATURAL BORN KILLAZ

"needed to be three steps ahead of the game and that mean get an education and a diploma." John crew barely understood what he meant, but they stayed in school.

CHAPTER 14
BRAZY B

December 1995

News had got around that the hair salon was laid down again, this time the culprits were Brazy B and the Bloods. Since Killa had played Brazy with the information that Charlie had given him, he had fallen for Killa's set up. Brazy put Killa and Red Flag's statements together which, made him decide to take Sandra out. He waited outside the salon in his Lincoln Towncar; with him were Bay-Bay, Bool Aid, and a Blood named Spider. It was expected that Sandra would be in the salon gossiping as usual. They waited. They waited so long that the plan Plan A was making them all frustrated. traveled fast, Brazy B soon heard about the retaliation and he was hotter than fish grease. He walked into his Pasadena suburb house and slammed the door. He crew.

Plan A had been organized out of respect for Red Flag and his wife. Brazy decided to wait until Sandra walked out of the salon opposed to going inside to retrieve her. It seemed like a good plan at the time, but it wasn't working for she remained firmly stuck inside the establishment and Bay-Bay was frustrated. "Da-damn Blood!" he stuttered. "This is-is not workin'. I'm too big to just be-be sittin' in this-this hot ass car witchu' nig-niggaz."

Brazy shook his head. His lil' brother was right! The car was stuffy and the sun shining into their eyes was not making things any better. However, he wanted to wait before considering plan B.

NATURAL BORN KILLAZ

Sensing the restlessness of his crew he snapped, "Bay-Bay, shutta fuck up! If yo' fat ass stop eatin' er'thing momma cook, you wouldn't have this problem!" Silence filled the car. It was so quiet Brazy drifted off into his thoughts.

Sandra did not attempt to contact him since Red Flag checked her about talking too much. He knew she was smart, but what he didn't know was she decided to keep a low profile after the night Red Flag had checked her. Brazy was so deep in thought that two hours passed and he was finally bought back to reality at the sound of Bay-Bay's and Bool Aid's huffing and puffing. They were sweating like two Sumo Wrestlers on a hot summer's day. They were sitting at a ninety degree angle and the California sun was blazing through the car turning it into a sauna. Irritated from the heat and the wait Bool Aid hissed, "Fuck Blood!"

"This bitch Sandra aint comin' out, let's go to plan B."

The waiting game had also got to Brazy and the thought of Sandra back stabbing him made him snap, "Fuck it! Come on."

Plan B was now in motion and it seemed simple, all they had to do was enter the salon and grab Sandra. However, plans often go wrong. As soon as they had entered the salon with their pistols drawn, Shante screamed, "Oh shit! What we do now?"

Shante knew who they were looking for but played stupid.

Honey Cuti, who thought of Shante's shop as her second home said, "Damn, Shante! Why every time I come to yo' shop some niggaz come runnin' in with guns?"

Shante's eyebrows shot towards the ceiling, "Bitch 'cause you always here when they come! And it aint like you ain't always here because bitch you sho' aint no customer." Brazy stood in the middle of the salon looking around, "We aint here to start no shit. We just here lookin' for Sandra."

TERRY WROTEN

Shante threw her hand up in a wild gesture, "Well, she aint in here. I aint seen her in a while. She might be hidin' out somewhere —"

Honey Cutie wanting some of the attention on her cut Shante off, "Can y'all be civilized and put dem damn guns down?"

Bay-Bay snapped. He was frustrated with the way everything was falling out of place. "Bitch, sh-shutta fuck up! Its bitches like you who-who think they can just talk shit. Bitch do-do you know how ta-ta spell civil-civil-civilized?"

Honey Cutie looked at Bay-Bay and shrugged her shoulders before laughing,"Ha!

Fat Boy, do you? Because you sho' can't say it."

Bay-Bay exploded! His face turned red and his grip on his .357 tightened. His insecurities over his speech impediment and his obesity turned into a murderous rage. He pointed his gun directly at Honey Cutie's face.

Honey Cutie wasn't afraid. In Nicholson Gardens, where she had grown up, she was robbed, jumped, raped, and stabbed; she had been through it all. She just sat with a fake smile on her lips and a look on her face that read: *Nigga if you're gonna shoot, go right ahead.*

Today, she was out of luck because that's exactly what Bay-Bay did. Shoot. He let off two rounds. Blah! Blah!

Honey Cutie dropped to the floor.

At the time, the hood's anthem was "Murder Was the Case," by Snoop Dogg. With all the sisters, ghetto queens, and hoodrats in the salon, Bay-Bay was destined to catch a murder case. If Brazy hadn't been quick on his feet that day, knocking Bay-Bay's arm upward, Honey Cutie's brains would have been spread all over the salon. She was lucky, the bullets only knocked off half her weave, giving her a mere quarter of an inch to spare.

NATURAL BORN KILLAZ

It was understandable that all the women in the salon panicked, and in the mist of the mayhem and screaming that followed, Brazy snatched the gun from Bay-Bay. "Nigga are you crazy?"

"I toldchu, you need to stop worryin' about what muthafuckas say aboutchu'. But since you rather be in jail for killin' a bitch that ain't worth a dollar, take yo' ass to the car."

Brazy shook his head, he was heated. He did not intend to disrespect the women in the salon, but things had got out of hand. He ordered his three Lieutenants back to the car and when they left he apologized to Shante and her clients. After promising some peace offering in the way of food and drugs, he left the salon.

Back in the hood, after handing Spider $500 to accommodate Shante and her customers, Brazy had Bay-Bay disciplined for his stupidity. Bay-Bay had been foolish and Brazy couldn't let that sort of behavior slide. He knew that if he did, his other soldiers would try to get away with other unjustifiable acts.

Brazy spent the rest of the day in search of Sandra. He hit every spot she was known to hang at, but she was nowhere to be found. It was obvious to Brazy that she had gone underground. He also knew that no matter how far she had gone, there was one thing of which he was certain, and that was it would only be a matter of time before she resurfaced.

As he lay in bed that night, his thoughts were only for finding her; but he could wait. Brazy was good at waiting. A snide grin spread across his face, and in the darkness he murmured, "You can take the bitch out of the hood, but you can't take the hood out of the bitch!"

"She'll be back."

CHAPTER 15

ECSTASY

1997

When John reached the age of seventeen, he decided to move out of Mama's house. It was time for him to pursue his own destiny, so he bought a two bedroom house around the corner on 42nd Street and Central. Not to be outdone, Kev bought a house on the borderline of the Crips and Bloods territory. His house was located on Hooper and 42nd Street, not too far Jefferson High School and down the street from Killa Black's house.

The two young Crips commanders decorated their houses with all the finer things in life money could buy: plush carpets, big screen televisions, Italian leather couches, silk curtains, crystal glasses, king size beds, and ornate china cabinets. The money was wisely spent according to John and Kev, considering they were expected to throw elaborate house parties. They organized invitations that read:

<u>You Are Invited...</u>
To KB's, KK's and the Gangs
Party.
<u>Everyone Welcome!</u>
Come and have fun.

The invitations for the parties were mailed or hand delivered, the first two parties were held at Kev's crib since it was closer to the school. The parties were popular and the crew made plenty of

NATURAL BORN KILLAZ

money selling drugs. Donita and Meosha served the liquor and also made a big profit. John and Kev had took care of everything else, serving all the popular illicit drugs on the market.

The success of the first two parties bought on the third party which was held at John's crib. Around this time, everyone in the crew had all experimented with smoking weed. Chronic was the main drug of choice, but the drug that was taking the hood by storm was Ecstasy. Ecstasy went by the street name of Thizzles. It was a small pill made with a mixture of various drugs. It was considered a party starter and everyone who attended the parties were popping them and getting high and horny. Previously, John or any of his crew tried Ecstasy, mainly because Killa had outlawed them from using the drug. However, after resisting temptation for so long, they joined the party.

Juvenile's smash hit *"Ha"* was blasting through the speakers when John popped his first pill. As Kev popped his, the party goers yelled "GO!"

Even though John popped his pill a few seconds before Kev, they both experienced an instant high and head rush. The cocaine that was mixed in the pill went straight to work. They wanted more.

The crowd went crazy as they popped yet another pill. It surprised everyone when "Miss Ghetto" swallowed one after swearing to never pop a pill. Meosha and Donita were standing strong after John and Kev fell weak to temptation, but like most brothers in the hood, they pulled their women down with them. John and Kev insisted until the girls submitted. Pressuring them to try the drug was one of the worst things both boys could have done, but at the time it didn't bother them one bit. They were having fun and being rebellious as usual. As the old saying goes ,"Young, dumb, and full of cum".

TERRY WROTEN

After Meosha succumbed, Donita followed suit. She was reluctant, not wanting the drug in her system, but she was under a great deal of peer pressure. She swallowed a Dolphin and drank a lot of water. Dolphins were the name of the pills they had taken that night. As thizzles would eventually spread through the hood, various kinds and brands would surface.

Later that night, when the party was over and everyone had gone, Donita and John popped another Dolphin. They had sex nonstop and swallowed pill after pill while taken pulls off a Swisser Sweet blunt. The next morning, thizzles and sex was the only thing on their minds. Ecstacy was their new drug of choice and it immediately took its toll.

~~~~~~

As the weeks went by John and Kev hustled and went to school. They were now sprung off Ecstacy and it was costing them around $2000 a week. Word eventually reached Killa and he fell in tears. The hurt and anger that he felt was not only directed towards them, but he also blamed himself. He felt that led them astray and his conscience was killing him. Not knowing how to express himself towards them over the issue without causing any more damage, he decided to sleep on it and discuss it with Ebony first.

John and Kev had being using the drug for over two months and were continually horny from the drug. Donita was John's Queen and future wife as Meosha was Kev's, but the two young horny-intoxicated Crips started to find comfort in other women; in a bid to keep pace with their sexual appetites. It was not until they were caught, that they decided to kick the drug. Better yet, slow down.

Donita and Meosha yelled, "Aww hell to the naw!" when they walked in on them cheating. They were high as the Trump Towers. John was so high he was stroking Faith, a cheerleader, from behind and calling her Donita. Kev was on the other side of the bedroom

NATURAL BORN KILLAZ

receiving head from a cheerleader named Georgia. Donita and Meosha barged in so fast, John nor Kev knew what to do! They beat Faith and Georgia like runaway slaves, then turned their anger towards John and Kev. It took all of John's strength to calm Donita down and when he finally succeeded; his house looked like a tornado had hit it.

John had dodged every lamp, crystal vase, and chair in that house. Donita was mad as hell and he could have sworn he saw the devil blazing in her eyes.

Later, after the worst of her anger passed, she left. No amount of begging on John's behalf could change her mind. It was too late! He had done the wrong thing and his guilt and shame was relived when Miss Jackson arrived.

Hopping out of her car and barging into the house, Miss Jackson yelled, "John, I toldchu! I toldchu not to hurt my baby. Boy, what's the hell wrong witchu? What she ain't good enough no more?"

John tilted his head towards the ground and did not say a word. He knew that he had messed up. He stayed quiet and just watched as his first love and her mother drove off. Realizing the devastation he had caused, he slammed his fist into his palm. "Fuck!" he blurted. Mama always told him "you never miss a good thing until its gone".

As the weeks passed, John got high all day not caring that he was wasting a precious time in his life. Donita no longer called or came around. He felt like a wounded soldier who could not go back to war, and as much as Donita loved him, her pain would not allow her to call. At school, she did extra work and tried her damnest to act as if he never existed.

She popped pills and got high before school, during school and after school. What made it worse was that everyone at school knew they were having problems, even the principal. Mr. Perry attempted to get them in his office together, but when Donita saw John sitting in his office, she turned on her heels and walked away. She had not been able to accept the fact that John had cheated on her; plus she had other concerns, Donita was two-months-pregnant. She was in a dilemma, she did not know what to do, or how to tell John.

Things were no different for Kev and Me-Me, who remained separated. John and Kev had caused a split in both of their relationships. After months of messing up, Kev bought John and himself back to reality.

One day out of the blue he said, "John, we need to stop this shit! All the homies ain't approvin', especially Killa. We losin' mo' money than a legitimate business going bankrupt. We are losin' our girls and we losin' our families. Cuzz, we need to get our shit together and stop usin' our own supply. We gotta be some leaders not followers"

Kev's speech was John's wake up call. He was in one of the worst slumps of his young life. He was sprung off Ecstaxy and he needed to stop. He vowed at that moment never pop a pill again. Kev did the same. It was time to start over and come new.

CHAPTER 16
DONITA-KILLA

Donita cried all day after the doctor informed her she was two-months-pregnant. She had hoped that it was all a bad dream, that something else had happened with her body, and that she would be all right. Now it was official. She was pregnant and did not have a clue about what to do. She did not have enough strength to talk to John, so she went to Killa. She had seen how he listened to John's problems in the pass and knew he would be understanding. She arranged to meet Killa and Ebony at Mama's house, and Mama immediately sensed something was wrong.

"Benjamin, what bring y'all over here?" Mama asked, "It aint my birthday or a holiday, so what's the problem?"

Mama paused and a stern look grew on her face. She wanted to show that she was serious and as an afterthought, she pointed at Killa, "And if it's about John, I don't wanna hear about it. I cannot believe I let that boy get caught up in the White man's trap. I knew when I let him buy that house around the corner the devil had him hooked. He's so caught up, he got Donita out there with him."

Mama paused again; this for a while.

"Yes. Donita I know!"

The trio could tell that Mama was worried because she started pacing around the living room. John was killing his whole family,

NATURAL BORN KILLAZ

bit by bit, from the inside-out; but he was so into the streets he didn't realize he was creating his own destruction.

"Donita, I know, you, John and his little crew are all sprung off that poison the White man invented for y'all generation. First, they invented heroin, then crack, now what's it's called? Ecstasy or somethin'? Whatever it's called, y'all better stop before it's too late and y'all are dead!"

Mama did not let up. She kept going on and on until she had worked herself into such frenzy, that tears rolled out of her eyes. Killa had a hard time watching Mama and forced himself not to cry right along with her. Mama's words had hit him like a sniper aiming for a bull's-eye target. He felt guilty! Guilty from the past and for the present. All of the bad deeds and all of the wrong were fast catching up. At that moment, he realized what he was... he was a pawn. He wondered how in the hell did Mama know what was going on in the streets? He knew that if Mama knew what was going on, so did the LAPD. To him, it was only a matter of time before the streets got the best of him. He had become so lost in Mama's words that he could not speak on his own. He stuttered "Aaaaaaaaaaaaaaaagh..."

"Miss Wilson," Donita chimed in. She could see that Killa was having a difficult time and decided the problem was her's not his, "Miss Wilson, the reason we came over here is because I'm pregnant by John and there is another problem. I have been usin' Ecstasy for the past two months. I've been gettin' high since I caught John havin' sex with that cheerleader. But I need to stop 'cause now I'm pregnant."

As Donita explained her situation to Mama, tears filled her eyes along with everyone els3 in the room. Mama embraced her, as far as she was concerned Donita was her daughter. Ebony grabbed Killa as he broke down, a soft spot was uncovered within him and she knew it. He sat motionless as the drama unfolded.

When John came walking through the door, ten minutes later, he immediately noticed something was wrong. Donita ran to his arms and his only thought was for his queen. "What's wrong?" he whispered in her ears.

Donita wiped her eyes saying, "I've got somethin' to tell you, but I don't know how?"

"I think, I already know. But, first off, I wanna apologize for my mistakes. I promise, it won't happen again. And I swear I miss you like crazy."

Donita smiled, "I missed you too. But I gotta tell you somethin' serious"

Mama chimed in, "Go head child. Let it out."

After Donita told John the news, he blurted out loudly, "Oh Shit! That's what's up!"

Mama was not convinced because she interrupted saying, "Boy watcha mouth! You still ain't grown. What you need to think about is being a father, 'cause them streets and the White man goin' to eliminate that if you don't get your act together. And that goes for you too Benjamin."

Killa nodded in agreement. Her words were hitting home with him.

John looked at Mama and said, "Ma, as soon as we get enough money we're movin' outta the hood."

"And whachu call enough?" Mama countered.

Silence. John ignored her question. He had acquired over a million dollars and was planning to retire the streets at age 21. Mama did not know this and John planned to surprise her.

Killa, on the other hand, was starting to feel uncomfortable so he signaled for John to roll with him. John signaled back and gave Donita the keys to their house and his car. He told her to meet him

NATURAL BORN KILLAZ

at home. This was a mother's nightmare, John was lost to the streets like an addict to dope. He was gone!

~~~~~~

Later that night, when Kev arrived at John's house after a long day of hustling, he was surprised to see Donita unpacking her belongings. "Oh shit! What's happenin' cuzz? You decided to stop hidin', huh? Damn, you had both of us stressin' and I'm still stressin' over Meosha. Can you talk to her for me? Tell her I'm sorry and love her."

"She'll come around when she get over what you did," Donita said still unpacking.

Kev knew he had fucked up and didn't feel like being reminded, so he changed the subject, "Anyway where's Black?"

"He went somewhere with Killa. I think Killa is talkin' about movin' to Cuba. I was only ear hustlin', so I'm not for sure. But I do know he's givin' up gangbangin' and guess what?"

"What?" Kev asked. "John bought you a Lexus to get you to come back home?"

"No, crazy. I'm two-months-pregnant."

"Damn, the way you put it, I must be the last to know?"

"Nope, actually I haven't even told Me-Me. Matter of fact, I gotta call her."

Donita picked up the phone and dialed Meosha's cell phone but her phone just kept ringing, so she called Miss Thomas' house number. Meosha's mom answered and said, "Meosha is in the hospital. She is throwing up everythin' she eats. I think its food poison or stressin' over Kevin, or could be that she's pregnant!"

Kev and Donita arrived at Kings Hospital twenty minutes after the call. They walked straight into the emergency room and asked a nurse, "what room is Meosha Thomas in?" Me-Me laid curled up in the hospital bed asleep. Donita knew she had been crying from

TERRY WROTEN

the dry tears in the corner of her eyes. Me-Me's eyes sprung wide open as Kev placed a kiss on her forehead. Waking up to the sight of Kev bought chills to her body. She had cried all day at the thought of breaking the news to him. She was three-months-pregnant and it hurt knowing that Kev had cheated. She did not know what to do.

As she shivered Kev asked, "Whats wrong? And why you shakin'?"

After Meosha poured out her heart, Kev called John from the hospital. Jphn was with Killa on the Westside, and Killa was announcing his retirement. When John passed the news on to Killa Killa said, "See, I really gotta give this bullshit up! I'm bout to be an uncle not to one child, but two!"

~~~~~~

Two days later, Killa deactivated himself from the Crips' organization. He no longer used the name of Killa, leaving it behind and returning to his birth name. He was reputable in the Crip community and had earned every bit of respect. The homies applauded his decision and even though he did not want to hand everything over to John and Kev, he did and wished them well.

Mama smiled and cheered as she and Benjamin hugged goodbye. She loved the feeling of knowing Benjamin made it out of the hood alive and had escaped a jail sentence. She was so excited she kept saying, "Thank you Jesus!"

"At least one of my sons mad it out and get to see the light."

CHAPTER 17

By the age of 18, John and Kev were self-made millionaires. After Killa left, everyone in their crew was worth over a million dollars. They all held top ranks in the Crips' organization. Popa, Big Head, and Lil' Loco were the new Lieutenants who ran the drug operations, while Killa Black and Killa Kev supplied everyone. Money Mike became Lieutenant-General and third man in charge. He was moving 10 to 20 pounds of marijuana daily, nickle and diming and was reaping $300 to $500 a pound after his workers were paid. Donita and Me-Me gave birth a month after each other; motherhood was hard. They had to get use to staying at home fixing bottles, changing diapers, and keeping regular doctors appointments.

Don John Wilson was the name John named his first-born. He did not like the thought of having a junior, so he avoided naming the child after him. Instead, they shortened Donita's first name and used John's name as the child's middle name. Don represents leader, chief, boss, and head guy. John knew his son was going to be all of these characteristics so he nicknamed him Chief.

After Kev found out about Meosha's pregnancy, he was hoping that they would have a son. He wanted a junior so bad; he went to every doctor's appointment. When the doctor confirmed that the baby was a going to be a boy, he fell to his knees kissing Meosha's belly. He made it clear that Little Kevin was going to be named

NATURAL BORN KILLAZ

Kevin Thomas Goodman Junior, and on the day of his birth, Miss Goodman certified it when she shouted, "That's my grandbaby! He cries just like his father."

John and Kev shared a smile hearing this.

However, things did change. While Donita and Meosha stayed home taking care of their, John and Kev continued to go to school. They hustled and took care of the kids when the girls needed to go shopping or wanted a break. They all studied hard senior year. John and Kev bought lessons home for Donita and Meosha. All of them were scheduled to graduate with their class and it felt good. The temptation not to finish was a fight for John and his crew, but with Popa and his whole crew joining the Crips it took pressure off them. Popa's crew recruited day in and day out, calling their crew the *Hit Squad*. Everything east of South Central was becoming Crip territory and there was no stopping the Blue rage.

Rat was the new aspiring soldier for the Crips and Popa's right hand man. He was only 13, but was one of the coldest gunners the Crips organization. He had three murders under his belt and stayed on call hoping to add more. John quickly took him under his wing, because the police were locking a lot of the homies up and putting them under a great deal of pressure to talk. John did not want him to be caught like the other pawns. Rat was a valuable soldier and with Papa running the younger Crips, the Crips added another generation to their regime.

~~~~~~~

Time flew by so fast it seemed amazing that Don and Little Kevin were starting to walk. Don's skin was getting darker and Little Kevin was starting to look like his father. Prom was approaching, so they asked Jazz to baby sit. She was home on break and loved babysitting her nephews.

TERRY WROTEN

The night of the Prom, a super stretch limousine pulled up in front of Mama's house. The driver hopped out and opened the back door. Kev and Meosha climbed out. Kev was wearing a royal blue suit and Meosha a royal blue gown by Coogi. Mike and Carmen, the girl that he had met at the swimming poo,l looked like a million bucks. He was dressed in a money green silk suit, while Carmen wore a silk Prada forest green gown. Lil' Loco and Big Head dressed identical in navy blue Mr. Biggs suits, Stacy Adam's dress shoes, and Guess glasses. Donita and John had gone through the most fuss over their clothes. He wore a snow-white Armani suit, white gaters, and a snow-white brim. Donita looked stunning in a snow-white Gucci strap gown, snow-white stilettos, and a snow-white clutch. They all wore $10,000 chains that Killa had sent them as graduation presents.

Miss Goodman and Mama took pictures nonstop. This was the happiest day in their lives. John had never seen Mama with such a big smile, not even on Jazz's prom night. After Miss Goodman and Mama almost blinded them with the flash on their cameras, they went to Miss Jackson's house.

"Damn, cuzz, look at these slobs," Loco and Big Head blurted on their arrival. John had already discussed the event with Brazy on the phone, and he had taken it upon himself to ask could they stop by so Miss Jackson could take photos. It was not easy agreeing to a suicidal risk, but John knew Miss Jackson wanted them to come, and Donita kept begging. John had agreed, but not before, he paid the limo driver to stash five guns of theirs.

As they stepped out of the limo Donita's family and the Bloods cheered. Miss Jackson's camera worked overtime that night and Brazy B and Bay-Bay made sure the young Crips felt welcomed. John did not sense foul play considering the respect that the Bloods were showing. Even Bay-Bay walked over, gave him a hug, and

NATURAL BORN KILLAZ

whispered, "Even though yousa Crip, you still my lil' nig-gah. And don't you ever forget that General."

John nodded. He knew Bay-Bay was only letting him know that he knew he was calling the shots.

~~~~~~

Their next stop was the projects. It was risky. The Bloods could not stand them in their territory. Truth be told, they did not want to be in the Bloods' territory, but after Red Flag ordered all the Bloods to respect the Crips and Me-Me on her prom night, they couldn't abandon Meosha or her family. They had taken yet another risk and tempers flared as soon as they stopped to take photos. Someone yelled, "Fuck crabs!"

Loco looked around balled his fist and blurted, "Cuzz!"

John looked at Loco and Big Head, who were both heading back to the limo to the stash and said, "Now cuzz, let that slide."

This was their night of honors and congratulations, not the night for death and tragedy. They did not need a shoot out, especially in Blood territory.

They left the projects immediately after Miss Allen had taken photos and given her congratulations. Arriving at the Marriot, they made a grand entrance into prom. Donita and John won *best dressed* and Kev and Me-Me won prom King and Queen. John was mad because as far as he was concerned those titles belong to him and Donita. After the excitement of prom, they got ready for graduation. Eventually, all of them graduated with the rest of their class and it was like a dream come true.

~~~~~~

After so many years of attending school and doing hustling, John and Kev contemplated buying a few houses in the suburbs and enrolling into college. They were already successful in the drug game, so it was wise to add secondary schooling. It was time to get their shit together and become good role models to their sons, who were growing fast.

Their empire supported 30 workers who were bringing in money around the clock. The 10 crack houses they owned made over $2000 nightly. Money Mike's marijuana disturbution company was as big as the crack operations, so it became necessary to ask Jazz to open a few saving accounts for their children.

John did not hesitate depositing a million dollars into Don's account.

At age 19, John and Kev had become filthy rich. They had more bling than the Hot Boyz and more cars than Ford Motors. It's sad to say, "Nothing last forever", especially in the hood.

~~~~~~

It was Little Kevin's second birthday and Miss Allen called Meosha and asked her to bring Kevin Jr. over. John was at his house weighing some dope and waiting for Donita to get Don out of the tub. Miss Allen was demanding, so Kev decided to take them to her house. No one knew what Kev was thinking when he made this decision. Perhaps because the peace treaty was still in force he thought every thing would be fine. No one knew.

Meosha had never forgotten the time that Kev had walked her home. She had a bad feeling about him taking them into the projects. She assured him she could drive herself and that they would be fine, but Kev still insisted on going.

He said, "Damn, I said imma take y'all."

Meosha tried to protest, "But –"

"But What?" Kev snapped. "You act like you don't want me to see Miss Allen."

Kev was insecure. He thought that Meosha was cheating on him with someone in the projects. Ever since Kev had cheated, he had the crazy notion that Meosha would try to play catch up. Nothing

NATURAL BORN KILLAZ

Meosha could say would make a difference that day so she gave in to him.

"Fuck it Kevin! If you wanna take us that bad, come on."

That's when Kev called John. John was still at his house in the room weighing dope and putting money in his safe when the phone rang and Donita answered it,

"Hello!"

"Where Black at?" Kev asked.

"Hol' on," Donita said handing the phone to Don while she went to get John.

Don was anxious to talk on the phone and said, "Hell-doe!" His English was broking. He was still learning how to talk.

Kev chuckled, "What up Chief?"

Don answered, "My dad talk tu jew."

"Okay. Let me talk to him."

"Otay. Me love jew Uncle Kevin."

"I love you too," replied Kev.

John grabbed the phone from his son, "What's happenin' Crip?"

"Nothing much," he replied. "I'm bout to bounce over here to these slob-jects with Meosha. So I need you to pick up Little Kevin's big wheel from Sears and leave it at yo' house until the party."

John agreed, but was against Kev going into the projects. Somehow, he let his bestfriend talk him into picking up Kevin's present when he should have intervened. He should have said "NO!" Kev changed the subject so fast John did not get to speak against his better judgment.

"Hey cuzz," he said, "I see my nephew is gettin' bigger. He told Uncle Kev he loves me, that made my day."

For some reason John was not quick enough on the draw that day. Perhaps he was preoccupied counting money or perhaps he was daydreaming, but he fell for Kev's change of subject and said,

TERRY WROTEN

"I love you too. Shit, did I make your day also?"

Teasing him with those words was the last time John got to tell his best friend that he loved him. Kev hung up and took his family to the projects.

As soon as they pulled up in front of Miss Thomas' unit, Kev saw eight or so young Bloods staring. They were hanging across the street from where he had parked. Kev immediately checked his two .38s, placed on each side of his waistband. Then, he grabbed Little Kevin from his car seat and started walking towards Miss Thomas' unit.

Meosha's stomach fluttered from the situation. She hated the fact that she had not stood up to Kev's demands. She had wanted to bring her .25, but Kev denied her saying, "Hell naw! That ain't lady or mother like."

Kev had become very demanding after Meosha gave birth to Little Kevin. His insecurities were getting the best of him and often affected his poor decision making, like it did that particular day.

Walking to Miss Thomas' apartment, Kev felt the hatred and animosity coming from Red Devil and his crew. Red Devil was one of the young Lieutenants living in the projects at the time. His older brother was murdered the night John and Kev received their titles as killers. Seeing Kev in the projects was like a dream come true to this young goon.

Kev spotted Red Devil's flare and mumbled to himself, "Nigga, protect the family first, if anything go down."

Kev knew Red Devil was going to go against the peace treaty. Meosha also knew that Red Devil had revenge on his mind. She pleaded with Kev to take them back home, but he ignored her and began to contemplate his next move.

As they entered Miss Thomas' unit, he handed Little Kevin to his grandmother. Looking at Meosha's worried face he said, "Meosha,

NATURAL BORN KILLAZ

stop worrin'. We gon' chill for about twenty minutes with yo' moms and then gon' bounce back home".

Me-Me was not convinced and shook her head in disagreement, "Kevin, I know Red and Bear."

Bear was Red Devil's right hand man. He was his puppet and did whatever Red Devil told him.

"Them two bad-ass niggaz look like they were up to somethin'. I swear, I don't trust them. You should let me hold one of your guns."

Meosha felt hopeless. She hated the fact that she had not bought her gun. All of a sudden her knees began to tremble, her stomach fluttered, her heart pounded, and she broke into a cold sweat. Tears filled her eyes as she sensed danger.

"Meosha!" Kev yelled, "Calm yo' ass down. Them niggaz was just surprised to see me. So no, I don't need you to hold a gun. And stop all yo' panickin' and shit, we came to see yo' moms, not to worry about some niggaz."

Kev was being stubborn as always, so Me-Me sat down. She watched as Kev sat contemplating his next move. She imagined he was thinking how to get back up. Maybe he would call John, Popa, or Rat, she thought.

All of a sudden Kev hopped up, grabbed Little Kevin, and while cradling him in his right arm he gripped his .38 on the left side of his waistband. "Come on," he said knocking Me-Me out of thought.

No one could figure out why Kev did not take a few seconds to stop and call John. John would have put everything aside to come to Kev's aide. As much power Kev had in the Crips' organization, he did not use his head and this mistake became deadly. Perhaps, Kev was tired of running; tired of gangbangin', and trying to do his family thing.

As they walked out of Miss Thomas' unit, Kev saw something flash in the corner of his eye. Using his street smarts, he knew it was an ambush. In one quick turn, he tossed Little Kevin to Meosha and yelled, "Get back in the house!" He pulled out his .38 and started blasting. The sound of his .38 ricocheted throughout the projects; Red Devil didn't know what had hit him as every slug from Kev's pistol ripped into his flesh. Devil collapsed, his gun hitting the ground beside him, but while he was dropping, Bear was coming from behind Kev with two 9mm aiming.

"Kevin, watch out!" Meosha yelled as Bear started shooting.

The first two Teflons from Bear's pistol missed and gave Kev the chance to turn around. The third hit him in the chest as he fired back with his .38. Then, he ran out of shells and Bear kept shooting.

Boom, boom, boom,boom, boom, boom, boom, boom, boom, boom, boom, boom!

It was not until Kev had caught three Teflons to the chest that he realized Meosha had not ran back into the house. Slugs were flying over their heads. Kev gained enough strength to run and tackle them. As he laid over Meosha and Little Kevin, using his body as a human shield, Bear continued to shoot Teflons into him. Kev jerked and coughed up blood while he protected his family. With every once of life left in him, he made sure nothing happened to Meosha and his son.

After Bear finished his clip and ran off, Kev laid motionless on top of them. Meosha rolled him over hardly being able to face her nightmare. She started screaming for him to get up, but it was too late. He was gasping for his last breath. She leaned closer stroking his hair as he slowly and quietly said, "Me—Me—I—love—you. Take care—of—of—Kevin. I love—y'all."

Those were Killa Kev's last words and all that Meosha could do was cry as her first and only love died.

"Somebody help me!"

"SOMEBODY HELP PLEASE!" she screamed.

NATURAL BORN KILLAZ

Little Kevin was too young to know what had happened, but he knew his father was dead. He placed his little forehead on Kev's forehead and said, "Daddy I love you."

When Miss Thomas ran outside and saw Kev lying in a pool of blood with Meosha and Little Kevin next to him, she did not know what to do. She watched as Meosha cried uncontrollably then realized she had to get Kevin away from the traumatic scene.

~~~~~~

The news of Killa Kev's death reached John and the homies fast. After Miss Thomas called Miss Goodman, and Miss Goodman called Popa the whole hood knew. When Popa called John and told him of his best friend's death, his heart jumped out of his chest. John immediately hopped into his Mercedes and headed towards the projects. Tears rushed to his eyes when he arrived. John felt he left Kev for dead. He felt like a snake for allowing Kev to go into the projects by himself, and he did not want to believe that Kev was dead.

The police had the murder scene roped off in front of Miss Thomas' unit, and John saw the white sheet over Kev's body. Detectives Gilmore and Gilbert were chuckling from the thought of seeing Kev stretched out. John saw Gilbert lift up the white sheet and smile. He whispered to Kev, "You're not Killa Kev no mo'. You're dead Kev now." John read his lips perfectly and could not believe half the shit that he said. He knew they had a leak in their organization, but it was not until that day that it became a reality. John and Kev had never been in any kind of trouble with the law, so how did they know who Kev was.

"A snitch is puttin' salt in the game," John thought.

Gilbert stood over the bloodied sheet and barked, "This is what this nigger gets. He wasn't shit. He was a piece of shit. So hey! Another nigger bites the dust."

TERRY WROTEN

John almost snapped! He gripped his Colt 45 and fought back every bit of temptation. He wanted to shoot the brains out of his head. The only thing that stopped him was the thought of Donita and Don. Kev was gone and now it was up to him to shoulder all of the responsibilities. He cried involuntary tears of grief as Gilmore replied to his partner's statement, "Now all we've got to do is get that sonofabitch right there!"

Gilmore was pointing at John.

John stood behind the yellow murder scene tape with fire in his eyes. He knew the two White detectives didn't respect his gangsta or Crippin'. They looked at him as a pawn. He stared back at the two White detectives and all the other White police, and his animosity towards White people grew. They were all rejoicing over Kev's body and it was though they were chanting *"ding dong the nigger's dead, the nigger's dead, the nigger's dead."* Looking at them rejoicing, had taken his mind back to Mama's speeches.

"John, White people only use Black folks as pawns and try to brainwash us."

"John, there's only two places them streets will have you, in a cage or in a grave."

"John, prison is packed and it's filled with Blacks."

"John, gangs only destroy our race. They're like tribalism."

"John, please think! Use your head!"

"John, please!"

"John, please!!"

"John, please!!!"

John shook himself out of thought. Mama knew best and Mama's speeches were getting the best of him, but he had bigger and better things to do. He had to start contemplating his next move. The Bloods had killed his best friend and half his heart was dead as well. IT WAS WAR!!

CHAPTER 18
THE WAR

The morning after Kev's murder, Popa and Rat were laying low in a stolen Astro Van hoping to catch some Bloods slippin'. Hours ticked by before they worked out a plan of retaliation. They changed into red clothing and walked through the projects armed with two .45s and two .357s. As they walked, Popa turned to Rat saying, "Cuzz that's one of their spots right there!"

Rat grinned, "Well it's goin' down then."

It did not take long to come up with a plan. It was already staring them in the face. Once Popa stated a spot was in their presence it was *ride or die*. Rat gently knocked on the door, as if he was a member of the Bloods' organization, and the door was answered by an older gangsta.

Red Flag was caught at the wrong place at the wrong time. He was at the spot picking up money and dropping off supplies when Rat knocked on the door. Red Flag was caught slippin' when he answered the door without checking the peep hole.

"It's me Blood," said Rat.

"Who?" Red Flag asked as he opened the door.

Red Flag slipped and in doing so, it cost him, Little Scottie, and four other Bloods their lives. Popa and Rat took no prisoners. The first slugs from their guns blew Red Flag out of his misery. Then, they jumped over his body and continued their *Slaughter House*

NATURAL BORN KILLAZ

mission. Little Scottie along with Red Flag, were the only Bloods awake in the house at the time. He was up handling business with Red Flag over a game of chess, so he had no time to counter when bullets from Popa's .357 filled his chest.

As Popa pulled the trigger, tears rolled down his face and he hissed at Scottie, "This is for my brother, bitch!"

Boom, boom, boom, boom, boom, boom!

Meanwhile, Rat did not wasted time, running through the house gunning down anyone who moved. Every Blood in that house woke up to a tragic end. After the slaughter, Popa and Rat went on a rampage through the house and gathered up their money, guns, and crack. As they left the devastation behind them Popa spat, "Checkmate bitches!"

"This Crip here!"

~~~~~~

The Slaughter House was the name the media and the LAPD used for Popa and Rat's mission. After their killing spree, John received back-to-back phone messages from Brazy B and a few of other Bloods, who he had come to respect trying to apologize and to cease-fire. However, John was too hot to answer and too hurt to talk. He ignored all calls and sat in his Mercedes listening to "Trade War Stories" by Tupac and the Outlawz. The pleas to stop the war were ignored.

John was constantly both participating in missions and ending soldiers on missions. He was not about to short change Killa Kev by letting his murder slide. He played his role as General to the fullest extent and stayed up all night and all day with his troops. They hit every Blood sect in Los Angeles and Brazy B was not going to sit back and let him wreck shop. Brazy had to retaliate. He received word of the war while out of state. He found out where Sandra was hiding and went to Texas to kill her. While he was gone, he

TERRY WROTEN

left Bay-Bay and Bool Aid in charge, but when he returned, Bool Aid was dead and the war was on. He could not believe his ears when he learned the Blood's body count. At that time, it was a count of 10 Bloods to 1 Crip and he knew that the Crips, especially Killa Black, weren't satisfied. He tried to call the father of his only nephew to cease fire, but after Killa Black declined his calls, he snapped! He instantly began to think of Bool Aid, and how he basically raised him. He did not want a war, especially against a kid he had literally raised and watched grow up.

However, as much as Brazy hated going to war against John, he could not sit back and watch his soldiers die. He thought back to when Bay-Bay told him how Lil' Loco, Big Head, and Money Mike had killed Bool Aid. They crept behind Bool Aid and two other soldiers of his and took their lives. He was told Big Head had taken Bool Aid's life at point blank range, while Money Mike and Loco chopped the other two Bloods down with AKs.

Thinking about how they were hit, Brazy was angry and hurt. What hurt the most was he let Big Head, Money Mike, and Loco come over prom night. Not only that, but on the Westside Crazoe, Midget, and Midnight were killing anyone wearing red. He shook his head, massaged his temple, and shouted, "Fuck crabs!" He meant evert word of it.

The war was now official.

John survived day to day on madness. The hurt that pulsated through him, had him bent on revenge. He stayed away from home to keep the madness away from his family, not realizing his was neglecting his son, Donita, Meosha and Little Kevin. He stayed at LIl' Loco's spot and he had only one thing on my mind...a killing spree from East to West.

While he was staying with Loco, he discoved Loco was messing with Georgia. John did not approve and told Loco to watch her.

NATURAL BORN KILLAZ

He knew that Georgia was a snake. He realized this fact after Donita and Meosha had caught him and Kev when they were having sex with her and Faith. He knew she set up because she used her cell phone right before Donita and Me-Me came barging in. It was his belief that she called them.

As John sat smoking some Chronic and sipping on some Gin, while listening to Lil' Wayne's song *"Respect Us"*, Loco's cell phone went off. He hit the walkie-talkie button on his Nextel and said, "What's up?"

John turned the music down and heard Georgia crying over the speaker.

"Loco, can you please come get me?"

"Damn, what's wrong?"

"My brother and his homeboys just jumped me. They told me to tell you, they gon' kill you."

"What?" Loco countered becoming heated, "Where you at?"

After receiving directions, Loco fetched the keys to his Benz, then grabbed an extra clip for his tech-9, and checked the chamber. He popped a few pills earlier and was high and horny.

John put his blunt out, turned the radio of,f and questioned Loco, "Nigga, where you goin'?"

"You know it aint cool goin' to pick up a bitch at this time of night durin' a war."

Killa Black hated the fact that Loco was going to pick up Georgia. Killa had always taught them that females, especially sisters who were caught up in the streets, were not to be trusted. He knew Loco was a pussy hound but he was surprised when Loco said, "Cuzz, I'll cee cack."

Loco was just like a brother to John so he knew there was no changing Loco's mind once it was made up.

TERRY WROTEN

Killa Black did not want to argue over the situation, especially after Loco had popped a few pills. Being buzzed himself off the Gin and purple, Killa Black figured the best thing to do was to roll with his boy, "A'ight, cuzz imma roll witchu'."

"Naw cuzz!" Loco protested, "Imma push by myself."

Since John had been through the same kind of situation with Kev, he was not too fond about letting Loco leave by himself. He ordered Big Head to roll with him. Loco refused and protested again, "Naw cuzz! I don't need cuzz to ride with me. I'm a grown ass man!"

Killa Black became frustrated. He did not want Loco to go alone, but he could not force a man to do something he did not want to do. He said, "A'ight cuzz, if this is what you want, do you? You high off them pills and pussy whipped. Nigga, you can't turn a ho' into a house wife."

"Whatever cuzz!" Loco replied. "I'll holla atchu when I get back. You still my nigga, but I gotta go get me some pussy. So don't hate."

Those were the last words John ever heard from Loco.

Loco walked out of the spot, hopped in his Benz, slid in his *"Last Meal"* disc by Snoop Dogg, turned up his system and played, *"Wrong Idea"*. John stood looking out of the window shaking his head as Loco placed his tech-9 on his lap and drove off.

Loco was Killa Black's Lieutenant, his boy, his brother, and his roll dawg. He was gunned down ten minutes later. He let Georgia betray him for $5000. Killa Black had known all along that she was a snake, so the money she made went to Loco's mother. She did not need it anymore because he killed her the next day, but not before she told him how she and the Bloods had murdered Loco.

~~~~~~~

Brazy B ordered his troops to find Loco, Big Head, or Money Mike when Spider said, "Blood that nigga Loco fuck with my nigga

NATURAL BORN KILLAZ

"What!" Brazy blurted, surprised because Sandman was one of his young soldiers who was loyal and worthy, "Put that on Bloods!"

"On Bloods!" Spider replied.

Sandman chimed in standing next to Spider, "Nigga, my sista'll do anythin' if the money is right. She'll suck the hair and skin off a dog's dick, if the money is right."

Brazy rubbed his chin. He had a plan.

Within the next hour he along with Bay-Bay, Spider, and Sandman sat in his 2000 Tahoe anticipating murder. They intended to kill Loco and paid Georgia $5000 to set him up. She met him in a parking lot at the Baldwin Hills Plaza. It was after one in the morning, so the Magic Johnson Theatre was closed and the parking lot empty. The only lights that lit the area were from Fatburgers, located down the street not too far from where they were parked. They instructed Georgia to wave when Loco arrived and then run into Fatburgers.

Their plan did not go as predicted. As always, no plan is perfect. When Loco pulled up, he knew that something was not right; he could tell by the way that Georgia suddenly ran off in the direction of the restaurant. It was at that very moment Brazy's tahoe was angling him in. Loco instantly thought "ambush"! He immediately blasted three shots from his tech-9 before Bay-Bay or Sandman could begin spraying. The three shots he managed to get off hit Spider in the neck, and he immediately died in the passenger seat of Brazy's truck. Brazy jumped out of the driver's seat while Bay-Bay and Sandman leaned out of the window spraying. He stood directly in front of Loco's Benz and let every slug he had go through the windshield.

Loco was ambushed that night; a snake betrayed him. He was hit with over a hundred rounds and had to have a closed casket funeral. Brazy dropped Spider off at his mother's house with $50,000 on his

TERRY WROTEN

chest. The Tahoe was found on 112th Street and Central across the street from the Nicholson Gardens in Watts. Brazy did not care much about what had gone down. To him, it was *Ride or Die*.

~~~~~~

Killa Kev , Loco , Little Crazoe, and Demarco's funerals came and went. Lil' Crazoe and Demarco were from the Westside and were killed at the Beverly Center. They were also set up to get ambushed by a snake named Candy. Their deaths happened the day Killa Black dumped Georgia's remains in a dumpster. When he cleaned that dirt from his hands, he proceeded to the basement where the Crips were having a meeting for ieutenants and generals. When he arrived, they got down to business. The only person that didn't show up was Lil' Crazoe.

It was three days before his seventeenth birthday when Lil' Crazoe and his twelve-year-old cousin Demarco decided to go shopping for FUBU outfits and some Air Force '1s. The war was claiming many casualties, so they decided to hit the Beverly Center. The Beverly Center was outside the hood so they just knew it would be safe; especially with the way Beverly Hills Police and the LAPD patrolled each and every block surrounding the area. As they hopped in Lil' Crazoe's 2000 Denali, his cell phone rang. Looking at the caller ID, he smiled. It was Candy his girlfriend, whom was several years older than he was.

He answered on the first, "What it do, boo?"

"Nothin' much, just chillin'," she replied. "Baby where you at?"

"I'm at the house hoppin' in the truck. Me and Demarco bout to go to the mall. Why, what's up?"

The meeting was over around this time, the Crips mainly discussed Killa Kev and Loco's deaths. John's heart pumped a hundred miles an hour during the meeting. He could not figure out why, but he would eventually learn that it was because he was sensing

NATURAL BORN KILLAZ

learn that it was because he was sensing another one of his soldiers was in the process of being murdered.

Exiting the basement, Crazoe pulled Killa Black to the side. He told him he felt something was wrong with his brother and he needed someone to roll with him.

Killa Black agreed and Crazoe said, "Hol' on."

Crazoe stepped to the side and dialed Lil' Crazoe's cell phone. He answered on the first ring.

"Where the hell are you?" Crazoe snarled into the phone.

"Oh Shit!" Lil' Crazoe blurted, "I forgot all about the meetin'."

Crazoe ignored baby brother again asking," Where the hell are you?"

"I just picked up Candy, and we're on our way to the Beverly Center."

"What?" Crazoe snapped, "Nigga, where is Demarco?"

Crazoe was livid. The Crips established a set rule for the gang. This rule was against being out and about while bullets were free falling. Crazoe told his brother on many occasions to stop hopping in his truck to go flaunt while the war was on, but Lil' Crazoe was too young and wild to pay attention.

Finding out that Demarco was with him Crazoe asked, "Do you have yo' burner?"

Lil' Crazoe replied, "Yep."

"Well, meet me at the house when y'all come back."

Killa Black looked at Crazoe as he closed his phone. Crazoe was boiling hot and stressed. Killa Black decided to have Popa and Big Head roll with them, there was no telling what trouble they were destined to get into with Crazoe being so angry. They all leapt into Crazoe's new Suburban armed and dangerous.

The whole time Crazoe was on the phone, Killa Black was wondering if the Candy, Lil' Crazoe had with him was the same Candy that Kev had lost his virginity to when they were eleven. If so, it was not good.

He asked Crazoe, "Is that Candy Beasley?"

"Yep." Crazoe anwered, "How you know that?"

"Damn!" Killa Black blurted. He knew thsy bitch Candy got around and was a hoodrat. He knew not to trust her with anybody's life. He felt hopeless because the same feeling he felt when he seen Kev's body under that white sheet came over him. Death was near and he felt it.

"Cuzz, that bitch aint cool!" he yelled smashing his fist into his palm. "That bitch has been a hoodrat and snake before me and Kev even started bangin'. Matta of fact, Killa told me the deadliest piece in this game is a bitch like Candy. And now that I think about it, she's been fuckin' with them niggaz off 33rd for years."

Before Killa Black could finish his sentence, Crazoe was busting a U-turn,

"Cuzz, I felt it!" he panicked, "I felt it!"

Crazoe picked up his cell phone and dialed Lil' Crazoe's number, while traveling sixty miles an hour down La Brea toward the Beverly Center. As they flew down the busy main street like felons on a getaway he shouted, "Fuck! Cuzz not answerin' his phone!"

Crazoe and Killa Black both sensed and smelt Lil' Crazoe's death before them, and they were trying their hardest to prevent it. At the time, their theory did not make any sense to Popa. He sat in the back seat saying, "Man, yall niggaz trippin'! My brother's and Loco's murder got y'all trippin'."

Lil' Crazoe, Candy, and Demarco finally arrived at the mall. It was set in Lil' Crazoe's head that he was going to stop in every store in the mall to surprise Demarco. Demarco was only twelve; he wanted to surprise him with an X-box.

NATURAL BORN KILLAZ

However, Candy did not care about video game shopping. She had other plans and wanted to hit Normstorm. She begged Lil' Crazoe to go against his original plan, "Please Dontrell, I don't wanna go to no damn game store. If you go, I'm leavin'."

Lil' Crazoe snapped, "Bitch, you asked to ride with me, so if you wanna bounce, bounce!" Candy was working his nerves, but what he did not know was that she was being paid to be an infiltrator. She was setting him up and was trying to come up with a plan to get away from him. Her plan worked and she spat back at him saying, "Well since you sayin' it like that, bye!"

Lil'Crazoe felt his temperature rising. He was becoming more upset by the minute, "Fuck it bitch! Fuck on then!"

After Candy disappeared through the mall, Lil' Crazoe and Demarco made their way to the game store. They had not been there long when four Bloods entered with red flags in their back pockets. Lil'Crazoe's heart dropped, but he was not blued up, so he thought the Bloods were probably doing some shopping like him. His only worry was that he allowed Candy to talk him into leaving his glock inside his truck,'Fuck!' he thought. " gotta go get my burner.

"Come on Demarco. I forgot my wallet. I left it in the truck."

They walked out of the game store and the Bloods followed. "Damn," he cursed. He grabbed his cell phone to call Crazoe,but was cut off by four more Bloods who emerged from the entrance of the mall. He knew they were in the middle of an ambush.

"Demarco, run inhat shoe store over there and stay there until I get back."

Demarco did as he was toldd. He took off toward the shoe store and Lil' Crazoe kept walking. He was hoping that the Bloods would only follow him, but they not only followed him, they also went after Demarco.

TERRY WROTEN

Killa Black, Crazoe, Popa, and Big Head were pulling up at the back entrance when they saw Candy speed walking out of the exit without Lil' Crazoe or Demarco. She spotted them and became startled. Crazoe blurted, "Bitch, where is my brother?"

Candy knew that she had was busted, especially after leaving without Dontrell. Tears immediately filled her eyes. She knew death was upon her. She stuttered, "Crazoe—Crazoe the Bloods..."

"The Bloods what?" Crazoe snapped.

"The—Bloods—are—in there."

As soon as Candy started talking, Killa Black's heart dropped. He knew she was a snake and the only thing he could say to her was, "You triflin'-ass- bitch..."

Before he could finish his statement Crazoe's .357 went off. Boom! Boom! Boom!

Candy slumped to the ground and Killa Black mumbled, "Damn." They were in the suburbs, on the borderline between Los Angeles and Beverly Hills, and Crazoe did not give a fuck. Even though it was a spontaneous act and prison was written all over the scene.

The quartet of Crips ran into the mall with their guns out and blue rags over their mouths. The shoppers went crazy, thinking it was a robbery. As the alarm went off, they spotted four Bloods ushering Demarco towards the front exit. It was over two hundred yards away and they had Demarco in a headlock. He had tears in his eyes as he was trying to break loose. In his bid to break free, he fought so hard that they picked him up by the arms and legs.

The scene became chaotic when Crazoe started running towards them. The Bloods immediately spotted him. They dropped Demarco and put two slugs in his head. As he fell tears rushed to Killa Black's eyes. He had been crying all week, but he cried more over Demarco. The kid was only 12!

NATURAL BORN KILLAZ

Crazoe shouted his name as he fell and all hell broke loose. The Crips were a hundred feet away from the Bloods, when bullets started flying. The Crips shot and the Bloods returned fire! It was a shootout and the only person that was using his head was Big Head. He grabbed his counterparts and yelled, "Cuzz, stop! Innocent people are gettin' killed!"

The Bloods made their way out of the front exit as armed security guards emerged into sight. Killa Black grabbed an emotionally distraught Crazoe, who was in shock from the sight of Demarco's dead body and said, "Come on Crazoe. We gotta go."

They were now a few feet away from Demarco's body and Crazoe would not move. He was in pain. KB grabbed his gun and again said, "Come on Crazoe. We gotta go."

Crazoe snapped into reality and the Crips took off toward the Suburban. They never came across Lil' Crazoe in the mall, and as they were making their miraculous getaway, he was in the process of being killed.

When Lil' Crazoe made it to the parking lot the alarm went off and he immediately thought of Demarco. The Bloods were still trailing him so he started jogging to his truck. As soon as he made his move, shots went off inside the mall; his thoughts instantly went to Demarco. He cursed himself, "Fuck!"

By the time Lil' Crazoe made it to his truck, Killa Black and the other three Crips were hopping back into Crazoe's Suburban. It was apparent they were about to be pursued because the police were right on their bumper. Then, all of a sudden, they turned away and headed back towards the front exit of the mall. It was also apparent that they were heading towards the Bloods and Lil' Crazoe. The quartet of Crips were relieved. They hopped out of Crazoe's truck three blocks down.

TERRY WROTEN

    Lil' Crazoe was not so fortunate, as he reached his truck he hit the alarm and reached under the seat to retrieve his gun, but it was too late. The Bloods filled his body with bullets. Lil' Crazoe got shot so many times, half of his body was in his truck and the other half laid on the pavement. It was not a nice sight.

    After the quartet of Crips made it back to the hood, Crazoe called his mother and told her the news. He wanted to tell her before the police, knowing it would be a little easier for her and his Aunt to handle. When word got back to all the homies there was so much anger, the war accelerated. It was the cause of so many deaths, the media and the public started rallying against gangs and gang violence.

~~~~~~

    The LAPD and every law agency in Southern California were fed up with the violence and nonsense created by the Crips and the Bloods, and filed a state of emergency against both gangs. When their self-destructing war made it out of the ghetto and a few tragedies happened in "rich-mans-land," they figured it was time to end the madness. Detectives Gilmore and Gilbert did just that. They were happy at first, when the Crips and Bloods were killing each other, but when the good citizens and the media got involved, they decided to call for help. They already had enough evidence to arrest everyone in the Crips and Bloods organizations, because there was a snitch operating amongst them.

    The detectives approached the court and filed warrants against the Crips and the Bloods. They were not concerned with segregating the two gangs while in the county. They knew if they took them all off the streets at the same time, they would eventually kill each other in jail. Before they arrested Killa Black, he murdered Bay-Bay.

NATURAL BORN KILLAZ

back. He was sitting outside of Loco's house with his Colt 45 on his lap. He stopped going inside the house since Loco's death, and found himself seated in the car in deep thought. It had been thirty days since Killa Kev's death, and Don's second birthday was the next day. He thought back to his younger days when he and Kev walked home and talked about what they were going to do when they got older. He thought back to the skating rink days, all the fights in the alley after school; even the incident when Kev got grazed by Lil' Scottie, and ultimately how Miss Nina saved his life.

He stayed deep in thought reminiscing over the old days amd savoring the memories of his best friend and their crew until he heard, "Damn, Blood, aint no crabs out." He stayed low and watched as a white Astro Van drove by very slow. The Bloods were inches away from having his head. At the time, he did not know Bay-Bay was in the vehicle, so he waited for them to drive pass. Then, he grabbed his 9mm from the stash and checked his .45. He hopped out of the car with both guns in hand and ran behind the van until he got within five feet.

He yelled, "Fuck slobs!" and started blazing.

Boom, boom, boom, blah, blah, blah!

Shot after shot rang out with vengeance and caught Bay-Bay and his crew off guard. The driver was Sandman and he lost control, smashing into a parked car. Killa Black did not stop shooting until he heard someone screaming, "I'm hit! I'm hit!"

The voice sounded familiar; it belonged to Bay-Bay.

CHAPTER 19

April 3rd to August 21st 2002

On the morning of Don's third birthday John was in bed with Donita, and Meosha and the boys were sleeping in Don's room. As he laid awake in a world of his own, he mentally checked himself for neglecting his family; especially Meosha who was taking Kev's murder hard. The thought of how he should tell Donita that he was responsible for her brother's death, hung heavily over him. It had to be done and as soon as he summoned the courage to say, "Baby," a loud boom shook the house. He was puzzled about what was happening, until it happened again accompanied by foot steps and a lot of noise. His house was being raided!

Killa Black knew never conduct business where he laid his hea, so he never kept drugs at his house. At that moment, all he could hope for was that his safe would not be discovered. However, this was more than a raid. His whole empire was in the process of being trampled to the ground. FBI agents and law enforcers from Southern California screamed and yelled, "Nobody move!" They swarmed over the house like angry bees and there was a deafening thud as the bedroom door was kicked open. Gilmore was the first to enter his room yelling, "Don't move motherfucker! Or I'll blow your head off!"

Donita screamed as he threatened to shoot. KB looked at her and said, "Baby don't trip."

NATURAL BORN KILLAZ

Killa Black knew never conduct business where he laid his hea, so he never kept drugs at his house. At that moment, all he could hope for was that his safe would not be discovered. However, this was more than a raid. His whole empire was in the process of being trampled to the ground. FBI agents and law enforcers from Southern California screamed and yelled, "Nobody move!" They swarmed over the house like angry bees and there was a deafening thud as the bedroom door was kicked open. Gilmore was the first to enter his room yelling, "Don't move motherfucker! Or I'll blow your head off!"

Donita screamed as he threatened to shoot. KB looked at her and said, "Baby don't trip."

He kissed her on the forehead before surrendering.

Gilmore looked at KB with a satisfied smirk spread across his face, "John Wilson, we have a warrant for your arrest for the murders of eight innocent people, including a twelve-year-old boy, in the city of Beverly Hills."

"Don't know whatchu' talkin' about dude. Call my attorney."

Gilbert's face was contorted. It looked as though he wanted to kill KB right there in his own house, "We also have warrants for you regarding gang related murders, conspiracy to commit murders, solicitation of murder, solicitation of bribery, solicitation of..."

Gilbert went on and on. He hit KB with everything in the book. Killa Black was thinking, "Damn fool, when you gonna stop?" as Gilbert read off the list.

They cuffed KB and dragged him to a patrol car. He felt hopeless as his son and nephew cried as they watched him manhandled by a group of police. As he was being dragged, Mama pulled up. She had arrived with Don's birthday presents. As she looked at her son, she broke down. Tears filled her eyes and all Killa Black could do was mumble, "Mama, don't cry."

TERRY WROTEN

Mama's worst nightmare had become a reality. The White man had taken another child of hers. Killa Black felt bad sitting in the back of the patrol car. He never imagined himself being busted. He only had a few more months before he was to turn-in his rags.

As he was being driven to Newton Police Station to be booked, Crazoe's house was being hit. That day the whole Crips' organization was destroyed. Their empire was trampled so bad it was as if Hurricane Katrina had hit them. The police did their job well, hitting every spot and every block in the hood. The only homie who escaped was Rat. He was in the grocery store when the police hit his grandmother's house. After their whole organization was locked up and booked they were assigned court dates.

Three days later Mama, Jazz, Donita, Meosha, Miss Goodman, Tameka, Miss Phillips and their loved ones filled the courtroom. Walking into court John saw Mama and Donita's eyes filled with tears. They knew he would be stressing. He never stepped foot in a courtroom or a jail.

The police also arrested Brazy B and the Bloods, so the war and heated anomosity continued behind bars. Not only being at war with the Bloods, but Killa Black was instantly recruited into racial warfare. The activities within the county jail were different from those on the streets. The Crips had to not only worry about the Bloods, Mexicans, Caucasians, and the police; they didn't know who to trust amongst each other! Everyone hated Crips, so Killa Black was in far worst danger behind bars than he had been on the streets.

He forced a smile to show Mama that he was alright, but his eyes were blood shot and stress was showing on his face. Mama blew him a kiss and signaled for him to pray with her hands.

He nodded.

"All rise! Judge Lance E. is presiding," the bailiff shouted.

NATURAL BORN KILLAZ

The judge looked around the courtroom before looking down at the case notes, then started calling names.
"John Wilson aka Killa Black."
"Donati Jones aka Crazoe."
"Michael Brown aka Money Mike."
"Tevin Goodman aka Popa."
"Michael Malone aka Midget."
"Wesley Jake aka Big Head."
"And Phillip Phillips aka Midnight."
"Will all seven of you please stand and raise your right hand."

John hesitated before raising his hand. He whispered to his state appointed lawyer, "What the hell he want us to raise our hands for?"

"Procedure", the lawyer whispered back.

At the time, John had not found a good enough attorney to represent him, and the state attorney representing him thought he was stupid. John was not going to raise his hand to the title Killa, and the other Crips weren't going to move until he did.

Ignoring his representation he interrupted the court, "Judge, my name is John Wilson. I don't know where you got that Killa Black moniker from but that ain't me?"

Instantly, the homies caught on and stated their names while they denied their aliases.

The judge rubbed his chin and said, "Okay guys, I'm just reading from the paperwork here in front of me. I'm not here to discriminate against you. There are forty-three of you guys, so I need to establish who is who. As it stands, the seven of you represented are documented to be the ringleaders of this gang. The prosecutor is requesting that capital punishment be enforced if you are found guilty. The charges range from capital murders to solicitation of firearms to the sale of controlled substances. It is also noted that

TERRY WROTEN

one of the ringleaders have not been captured"

After that statement, KB thought about Rat.

Then, all of a sudden the judge said, "Benjamin Wilson is noted to also be a ring leader. There is a warrant for his arrest, so when he is apprehended he will be arraigned."

John stared in disbelief at Mama, but she shook her head and stayed quiet.

The judge continued, "How do you seven plead to these charges before me?"

By now, sweat began started to trickle down John's forehead and the state appointed attorney witnessing his distress, turned towards the judge and said, "Your Honor, my client and the rest of these men plead not guilty and we ask that bail be set reasonably."

The judge hit his gavel and said, "Bail is denied! Due to the magnitude of this case and the status documented on each individual, there is a chance these defendants will flee. As of now these defendants are to remain in custody until a trial date is set."

The judge had denied them bail and Killa Black could not believe it. He wanted to cry. He knew he had officially signed his life over to the Devil, The White man. His life on the streets was over!

~~~~~~

John concentrated on fighting his case while he was locked up in the Los Angeles County Jail. He was placed in maximum security, and separated from everyone in his organization. He stressed for the first four months, adapting to the jail lifestyle, and it was hard. Mama, Donita, and Me-Me were present at all his court dates and visits. He had everything a prisoner could have. He read books and magazines to keep his mind occupied. As his trial date drew closer, his situation was not looking good. Crazoe wrote a letter to Donita saying Big Head was with an informat. He dismissed the claim. He knew Big Head, he had grown up with him. He figured the leak in

NATURAL BORN KILLAZ

their organization had to be Rat, considering he was the only one that had avoided arrest. There had definately been a leak, but the police had planted their decoy so well the Crips could not pin point who it was until trial.

Killa Black had found the best lawyer money could buy; a guy by the name of Jay Cooper. He gave Donita the code to the safe and she paid him in full to represent John. Jay Cooper had won over ten high profile cases, and the law firm he worked for carried the best attorneys in the state. He was Killa Black's only hope because his case was sliding down hill like an avalanche he needed a miracle.

The Jury consisted of eight Whites, two Blacks, one Latino, and one Asian.

Every day throughout the trial the courtroom was packed. Family members, friends, and loved ones of the Crips sat on the right, the media and the victim's families sat on the left. Miss Phillips was present every day of the trial, to support Midnight and John. She illuminated a strong presence on heir side. She was so powerful Jay Cooper commented, "Who is she?"

The Trial went better that most had expected, especially during the first few weeks. Even though several police officers gave daming evidence against the Crips, the prosecutor could not present any hard evidence against them. Everything was circumstantial until two days before he rested his case. He surprised the courtroom when he said, "Your Honor, the people would like to call Special Unit Undercover Officer, Wesley Jake to the stand."

"You bitch ass nigga," was all Killa Black could say. He could not believe he had been played that easily. He was dumbfounded! He had grown up with Big Head. It was not until that day he realized Big Head was the only surviving member of his orginal crew that was not on trial with them. He should have killed him while they were in jail, and he was still acting as an undercover agent.

TERRY WROTEN

Me-Me snapped as Big Head walked into court with his LAPD badge hanging from his neck, "Aww hell to the naw! You ain't no muthfuckan police! You'sa bitch ass nigga who cant take the heat"

The bailiffs rushed over to Me-Me and the judge shouted, "Order in the court!"

"One more outburst and you will be ordered to leave!"

As the jury sat startled from Meosha's outburst, Killa Black stared at Big Head as he walked to the stand. Big Head avoided looking at KB. He knew that he was as guilty as everyone standing trial was. Killa Black thought back to the Beverly Center when Big Head stopped them in the middle of the shootout. That was a sure sign right there, but KB was too ignorant to see it. He could not believe it! Their trial had been going well but all of a sudden, one of his boys turns out to be the police! He just shook hia head. The prosecutor did not make things any better when he called him, "Officer Jake".

"Officer Jake, can you please tell the jury and the court how long you have been a Los Angeles Police Officer?"

Big Head looked straight at John and said, "I've been an undercover officer since I turned eighteen. That would be about four years and three months."

Popa tapped Killa Black on the leg and whispered, "Cuzz been a pig since I was thirteen. No wonder they got Killa's name in the mix."

Popa was right. But the prosecution was far from over.

"How long have you been affiliated with the Crips?"

Big Head replied, "Well..." --he paused. Guilt was wrecking his conscious. "Well, I've been a Crip since I was fourteen. The only reason I joined was because at the time I felt the need to fit in. I was young and dumb and feared Killa Black and Killa Kev, who is now deceased..."

NATURAL BORN KILLAZ

"Donita told me," Was all Killa Black thought as Big Head testified against him. Thinking back to that day he risked his life to walk her home, he should have known Big Head was the weak link. He had missed the sign not to trust Big Head and he was hotter than fish grease.

The prosecutor interrupted my thoughts, "Can you please point to Killa Black?"

Big Head pointed at Killa Black saying, "Yes. That would be the gentleman right there, the one with his head down."

John tried not to look at his grade school friend as he pointed him out to the jury as a killer. It was not that he did not want to look, it was the hurt and anger that was welling up inside of him. The prosecutor walked confidently towards the judge and satisfaction was written all over his face as he said, "Your Honor, for the record, Officer Jake has identified John Wilson as Killa Black."

The Judge acknowledging the prosecutor said, "That will be on record."

The prosecutor went back to work. He made it known Big Head was first and foremost an officer not a Crip, and that Killa Black and his crew knew was monsters and notorious Crips!

"Officer Jake, can you finish explaining to the jury your affiliation with the Crips and the LAPD?"

"Yes. Killa Black and Killa Kev ran the school, everyone feared them even the teachers..."

"Objection your honor!" blurted Miss Phillips. "Excuse my interruption in these proceedings, but I will not sit through this and let a corrupt cop slander my character..."

The judge, prosecutor, the media, and jury were stunned! Who in the hell was this woman?

Miss Phillips filled them right in, "My name is Dr. Phylicia Phillips, and I was a teacher at Carver Middle School where most of the accused attended. I also taught Wesley Jake and John Wilson. And I can assure you there was not one teacher who feared any of these boys."

After Miss Phillipsspoke her peace, she was ordered not to interrupt the court again. She calmly sat down, but her presence was so powerful the prosecutor fumbled with his words when he told Big Head to continue.

"At age sixteen, I decided the life of gangbanging, killing, selling drugs, and fighting over territory was for low-lifes, so I joined the explores to become an officer. That is when I met Detectives Gilmore and Gilbert. My role as an explorer was to hang with the Crips, I would then, inform the department about everything that took place within the Crip organization. When I turned eighteen, I became the lead undercover agent."

Big Head was good at lying. He did not choose to become an explorer or an informant; he took a deal to become a snitch. It happened the year he was caught with tons of crack and guns, and as a result of the deal he made, he only served two weeks in juvenile detention.

"So Officer, just for the record, you actually hung with all five of these Crips?"

"Yes."

"Could you point them out for the record and the jury?"

"The gentleman on the far left is OG Midnight."

"The gentleman next to him is Crazoe."

"The juvenile next to Crazoe wearing blue is Popa."

"And the gentleman next to Killa Black is Money Mike.".

Big Head told everything that he knew. He told how Killa Kev was killed, and ultimately how his death had started the war between the Crips and the Bloods. He described how Bool Aid was murdered, but did not mention that he had pulled the trigger.

NATURAL BORN KILLAZ

He blatantly blamed Lil' Loco and Money Mike. He told how Killa Black had killed Bay-Bay and how Crazoe and Midnight masterminded all the murders on the Westside. He told how Popa joined the gang at age 10, and had been a killer ever since.

Mama sat with tears rolling down her face as Big Head gave evidence against her son and his friends, her extended family. She thought back to all the times she allowed Big Head spend the night at her house and the numerous times she fed him. She thought back to how she had to force Big Head and the rest of John's crew to go home at times. She was hurt. She also preached to her boys about the White man using young Black men as pawns, and Big Head was the best example. Like in chess, they pushed the pawn to get the king.

Donita could not believe that Big Head was on the stand spilling his guts. She had known all along that he was not what he claimed to be, but she never thought of him as a pig. Her stomach fluttered when he told the court that Killa Black had killed her brother. She passed Don to Jazz and walked out of the courtroom.

The five Crips standing trial sat staring as their weakest link sung like a bird. Popa was confused; he did not know what was really going on. He was only seventeen. Money Mike sat reflecting back to the night Bool Aid was killed, and how Big Head had executed that murder. Crazoe and Midnight stared, mesmerized by their new enemy. Crazoe was steaming because he warned Killa Black a long time ago that Big Head was no good.

Jay Cooper tried his best to represent John and his homies, but Big Head was excently trained for cross-examination.

"Where were you when all of these alleged murders took place?"

"I – I was in the crack houses waiting for them," Big Head lied again, stuttering through his answer. "Then, when they return they would tell me what had happened."

TERRY WROTEN

"So what you're saying is that you hung with these alleged murderers, but you were so privileged that you didn't have to get your hands dirty by going out and killing with them?"

"I stayed in the crack houses, making money, so I didn't have to go out in the fields..."

Money Mike snapped. It was only he, Killa Black, and Big Head left from their original crew, and Big Head was telling lies and exaggerating. He hopped out of his chair yelling, "Fuck that! Cuzz lyin'!"

Killa Black had to calm Money Mike down; the bailiffs were approaching and there were so many emotions flowing he knew that if they'd touched Mike it would have triggered a roit.

KB whispered, "Mike, chill out! Let cuzz play himself."

Mike looked at KB and shook his head as if he was saying, "Cuzz, imma kill this nigga."

The judge banged his gavel, "I will not tolerate any more out bursts."

Jay Cooper continued to cross-examine after everything calmed down.

"So Big Head, you admit that you stayed at the crack houses. You admit that you made illegal money, while everyone else left you there so they could go out killing and fighting over territory, am I right?"

Big Head answered, "Right."

Jay Cooper went in for the kill, "So you were the real mastermind of this organization were you? You admit to doing things only John Gotti and bosses of his kind have done. You sat clocking money while your soldiers were out committing all your dirty crimes. You then questioned their actions, like a boss, to see what had happened. So if anything, you're the real perpetrator, am I not right?"

Silence. Big Head did not say a word. He was caught in his lies.

NATURAL BORN KILLAZ

Jay Cooper continued, "You sit in front of this jury, saying everything you heard, or shall we say probably heard, since you could also be making these stories up, because how do we know you're not? How do we know that it's not you that's the real and admitted suspect?"

Big Head ignored the questioning again only balantly saying, "As I have already stated, my only participation was through association."

It was final. Jay Cooper had done his best. He had raised many issues in attempt to destroy Big Head's credibility, but Big Head was avoiding questions and saying things that never took place. He was a true LAPD officer and acted as though the Crips had never meant anything to him.

On Tuesday, the 21st of August, 2002, a week after the jury went into deliberation, Crazoe and Killa Black were found guilty and sentenced to death for all the murders in the Beverly Center. They received the death penalty because five innocent White people were killed that day and they said Crazoe and Killa Black were responsible. Popa was also found guilty for the Beverly Center incident, but since he was a juvenile when the crime took place, he received life without the possibility of parole. Money Mike and Midnight were found guilty but since they were not involved in the Beverly Center shootout, they received the same sentence as Popa. Midget never stood trial. The authorities killed him off with medication. He ended up committing suicide before their trial ended.

Two days after Killa Black's sentencing, he was flown by helicopter to his future home, San Quentin State Prison. Crazoe arrived a day after KB, but they rarely saw each other. Occasionally, they would catch a glimpse of each other when one or the other were being escorted to the yard or to a visit.

CHAPTER 20
THE AFTERMATH

Monday, February 4th, 2005

Killa Black woke up and was startled! He had fallen so deep in thought about his life he did not realize he drifted asleep. He rubbed his eyes, checked the time, and saw that it was an hour and a half after his normal 5:30 wake up program. He heard footsteps and a familiar voice at his cell door. It was C.O. Johnson with breakfast.

C.O. Johnson was around 45 years of ae. She was a correctional officer who KB had befriended. She acted strangely towards him during the first six months that he was on death row. This was understandable, considering he was going through the transition of realizing his fate. His first couple of months, he was still had the same attitude and gangbanging mentality. He needed to grow up, fast. Money Mike, Midnight, and Popa were killed during that time. They were incarcerated in the same prison and tried to escape. Popa was the only one who made it over the gate. He was shot with a Mini-14 slug to the head. He was dead before he hit the pavement. Guards shot down money Mike and Midnight before they reached the gate.

After Killa Black got over the grief and began to accept his situation, C.O. Johnson and he bean to small talk. After a year or so of pleasantries, they started seeing eye to eye, both seing beyond stereotypes and gaining a positive communication line. KB once thought everyone that wore a uniform was not to be trusted, and

NATURAL BORN KILLAZ

she thought the exact same way about gang members. It was good they were able to overcome their differences, because now she always stopped by his cell when she was at work.

As she opened the tray slot in his cell door, he hopped out of bed and saw a stack of mail on the floor. He knew the mail was slid under his door when he was asleep and so did she. Which raised the comment, "Wilson are you okay?"

Reassuring her he was okay she continued, "I've never known you to wake up this late? Why is your mail still on the floor? It looks like you have been asleep for days in there!"

KB did not feel like talking, especially with his morning breath not smelling the best. He grabbed his breakfast tray and told her that he would speak with her later after he finished eating and gone through his mail.

"Okay," she replied walking off.

Picking up his mail, he stacked the pile on his bunk, and then took a couple of bites from his tray. After seeing a letter from Donita, he was not hungry anymore. He put the tray to one side, walked to the sink, took care of his hygiene, and sat down to read her letter.

Thursday
January 31st 2005

Dear John,
I want to start this letter off by saying that Don and I love you, and you know we miss you sooo much. Meosha and Little Kevin also miss and love you. Me, Mama, Meosha, Jazz, Miss Goodman, and Miss Phillips went to put flowers on everybody's graves. I thought we were going to have to carry Miss Goodman back to Jazz's Expedition, because all of her son's are in the graveyard. But I was

TERRY WROTEN

wrong! Meosha was the one who couldn't take it. We literally had to make her pull herself together. After we left the cemetery, we went to Hometown Buffet and I know I shouldn't be food teasing you, but I'm just telling you about our ladies night out.

Oh yeah! Mama and Jazz bought a house next to ours. It cost a little over $2.8 million. It's similar to our house, but they got a bigger swimming pool and tennis court. Rat also bought a house out here and the record label is getting popular. He gave me an article from someRrap Magazine. I thin, it came out of the Murda Dawg or the Double XL. I really don't know, but I'm sending it to you to read.

Also, I ordered you a few more books, so let me know when you get them. I don't got much to say, because me and the family will be coming to see you this week. It probably will be a few days before you get this letter, but Jazz said she needs to talk to you as soon as possible.

Brazy told me to tell you, he sends his love and that he ain't mad at you no more on that Bay-Bay issue. You know he's at Tehachapi with one of Benjamin's lieutenants? I think his name is Dice. He got life on his third strike for possessions of sales. Brazy also said, "Always remember a man is made of hardship and should be able to survive and prevail in the lowest of situations, so keep your head up". He said, "Ask Allah to guide you and forgive you." You know he turned Muslim after getting all that time. My momma said with all the two hundred and fifty years he got, she don't know if Allah could help him. But she said you keep praying to God and something good will happen. John, she don't know that you have also been studying the Qu'ran and I'm not going to tell her.

Baby, did you know that Crazoe's son Dontai is clamin' Crip? I don't know if you seen Crazoe, but Tameka told me he getting out of control. And as much as I hate to say this, Momma said them tests came back and Don has a brother.

NATURAL BORN KILLAZ

John, I know it was a mistake, but you don't know how much you have hurt me. I can't believe, Faith's son is yours! He is only a couple of months younger than Don, so can you honestly tell me you didn't know he was yours? We will talk about it later, right now, I have to go get Don and Kevin from their private school. I don't wanna hear their teachers mouths because I'm late, so I'll talk to you later. But read Rats article and tell me what you think? I am so happy for him, he made it out of the hood.
Love your baby momma and wife,
Donita Wilson.

P.S. Enclosed are some pictures of our ladie's night and Rat's magazine article.

Killa Black read Donita's letter and felt relieved. He already knew almost everything she was writing about, but just hearing it from her was a breath of fresh air. Yes, he did know that Faith was the mother his other son Johatnan, but he never told Donita. He kept Faith on the side and made sure that she was straight. They say, what you do in the dark comes back to the light, so he ended up being caught. Eventually, everything worked out for him; and Donita accepted his son on that behalf. The boys will get to grow up together. However, KB had not heard about Rat's magazine article, so he instantly got to it.

KB had handed Rat the money to start his own record company after his trial. When he found that Rat was not the snitch, he told him to quit gangbanging while he was ahead. So with a well thought out business plan KB gave him the money. While opening the article KB smiled.It read:

TERRY WROTEN

Trued Up Records

Double XL goes behind the scenes with the youngest and most successful independent label owner on the Westcoast. So all you other record labels bow down to the R-A-T and his Trued Up Records.

From it's beginnings in a Los Angeles, California neighborhood, Rasheed Atkins Timley aka Rat story reads like a street novel. In the late 90's, a pre-teen Rat was governed and recruited by the Crips. A self-confessed ex-gangsta, Trued Up owner, has always preferred not to talk in public. Now that he's the last of what he refers to as the dying breed, he has something to say. Double XL has the exclusive with this young CEO. Rat sits on a grand plush settee in the living room of his newly purchased Malibu mansion. He is for the most part alone, but today, out back waiting on the grounds, Trued Up artists await their tour bus. Trued Up is on tour.

No matter how far in this world he has come, he is still what some would consider a boy from the hood, only now he could take his hood with him. He states, "All my boys are gone, so no need for all that."

Double XL: You say all your boys are gone, Clarify what you mean.

Rat: I mean what I said. All my boys are gone, my best friend is dead. He tried to escape from prison after getting over a hundred years, because a so-called friend of ours turned informant. Some Bloods killed one of the big homies, who raised me and took me under his wing when I was thirteen. My other big homey is on death row, so all my boys are gone.

Double XL: Tell us, what is your relationship with your big homey on death row, considering you're now a CEO?

Rat: Well, to be honest, I don't wanna put that over the air, just outta respect for my loved one. But I will say he's taken care of. All I can say is I wish he was here with me. His wife is the Co-Founder and

NATURAL BORN KILLAZ

President of Trued Up Records and her best friend is Vice-president. His sister is our consultant and accountant, so you could say that Trued Up Records is a family-based company.

Double XL: I heard some ruckus about a cop. Is this another case of LAPD corruption or what?

Rat: Basically yes! When the cops saw that they had nothin' on our crew they found a corrupted cop. That particular cat was worse than them cops on Biggie's case. The thing is, after the court case was over, the police let this particular dude walk. He was never on the police force like he claimed to be when he took the stand.

Double XL: So what you're saying is, was this guy played as an undercover cop at trial against your boys? But, and am I getting this right? Never was a cop?

Rat: This guy was a cop, but he still did all the real gangsta shit. He couldn't take the heat when they kicked in our doors. He let them play him, you know? Play the pawn to get the king type shit. But after they used this pawn, he didn't grow up and they left him for dead.

Double XL: Speaking of this cop being left for dead by LAPD, it was rumored on myspace.com that this fake cop or snitch was found dead two weeks after the trial and that Trued Up Records were responsible. Would you like to clear this up?

Rat: Hey look! Trued Up Records nor Hit Squad Management, had anything to do with that guy's murder. You gotta understand this case was all over the media, everybody knew this cat was foul. He was just a walking target. So to all them myspacers, or whoever started this rumor, come on y'all, don't bring the FEDS to my door. Trued Up is some positive shit, if it don't make dollars it don't make sense! Trued Up's motto is: a positive change is a positive plus. We aint with that bullshit no more. I'm only nineteen with two black cards, and I praise God and my big homey for my success, I don't

TERRY WROTEN

need that bullshit.

Double XL: It sounds like you're all about business, so could you contemplate doing business with a Blood or someone like Game?

Rat: Oh hell yeah! Game is hot! I like the dude. I believe in Robert Greene's 48 laws of power and law number two is very important if you're tryna make it to the top.

Double XL: And what's that law say?

Rat: Never put too much trust in friends and learn to use enemies. Greene's opinion is that a friend will betray you faster because they easily arouse to envy. He says, hire a former enemy and he will be more loyal than a friend, because the enemy will have more to prove.

Double XL: I see that you have been studying Robert Greene's theories real well, so are you telling me that you actually do business with dudes you once shot it out with?

Rat: Let me put it to you like this, I now have Bloods in my family. The Co-Owner of Trued Up has a brother who was a shot caller for the Bloods and war meant war with him. He's now one my consultants; he is in jail, but everything he lace me with be well thought out.. I don't discriminate; I just signed two ex-Bloods to a three album deal and their hotter than fish grease.

Double XL: For the record, what was the specific reason that decided you to turn in your rags and chose to go legit?

RAT: In the hood, I saw everything. I learned how to manage people and money because of my status in the gang. I had my followers, but I was a follower as well. I happened to have the best leaders one could ask for and when things went wrong, I was instructed to move on. I have always been a good listener, and I did exactly what I was told. Honestly, this lovely life I'm living is written on paper. I knew I was going to have 25 artists and a management company. I also knew that if I didn't stop gangbangin' I would now be dead or in jail. I once had a crew of Crips called the Hit Squad,

NATURAL BORN KILLAZ

half of them are dead or in jai,l and aint none of them over twenty. I swore that gangbangin' wasn't going to be a part of my life no more and moved on. So to all of them cats that's out there glorifying that bullshit, homie, that aint the life.

Double XL*: Well, I know you have to get going, because your tour bus just pulled up, but would you like to say something to Trued Up fans?*

Rat*: You know I gotta do that. First off, I wanna say to all Trued Up fans, we love y'all and we will be droppin' another album in due time, so stay loyal. Next, I wanna send a shout-out to my homie KB. Homie, I love you and wanna let you know that the family is taken care of. I'm living your dream and your plan, so thank you for your brotherly love and influence. Finally to Crazoe, stay up homie, I love you. Trued Up is out here and we're on the move. Tell Tamika she know what to do if she needs anything. I'm out!*

One Love

    Killa Black was smiling from ear to ear as he put the article aside. He felt elated Rat was the only survivor; the only one that had made it out of the hood. He knew that his family was safe. Rat seen to that. The death sentence looming over his head did not seem to be so pointless, now that Rat succeeded and that he had inadvertently made a positive difference in other people's lives.

    He picked up a blue envelope addressed to him from Terry Wroten and with trepidation read its contents. Terry was lucky, if Jazz hadn't spoken to KB the day before, his letter would have ended up in the trash, along with the other junk mail.

    After he read Terry's letter he smiled. He liked Terry's sales pitch. It was direct and to the point. As much as he hated talking about his life, he ended up thinking about Don, Johnathan, Kevin,

TERRY WROTEN

and their friends. He was obsessed about being a father since age fourteen, but by making the wrong decisions, he turned out to be a deadbeat. Now, he had nothing to offer and as a father who grew up being a fatherless child, he felt committed to telling his story. He did not want to leave his children like most fatherless children. He didn't want them to wonder how he looked, who he was, what he did, why he did it, or who he did it with. He knew all the things Mama told him about his father, but still wanted to know more, still wanted his essence. He wanted just to sit down with him and ask all those un-answered questions. So he knew by agreeing to let Terry tell his story that he would be able to help fill the blank for his children and help other children make better choices when it came to the streets and street life.

EPILOGUE
THE AUTHOR

Sunday, July 23rd, 2009

I sit here today at Central Juvenile Hall in East Los Angeles. I'm about to talk to the juveniles that are incarcerated here about life in general. I spent most of my juvenile years in this place, so most of the staff members already know my background. When I first signed in, the director handed me the Los Angeles Times and said, "I'm sorry your friend didn't win his appeal. This system can be corrupt at times."

I did not know how to respond, so I just nodded my head. I took the newspaper and walked to the gym. The staff had set up rows of chairs that were waiting to be filled by the juveniles that I would be speaking to. Walking in to the brightly lit gym Mr. Moore, one of the staff members who had been one of my Pop-Warner coaches greeted me, "Terry."

I nodded. "Wha's up, Moore?"

"Man, we're glad to have you come and speak to these young dudes. If you can change just one of their lives, we win!"

This was my first time back at the lockup facility where I had once raised hell. I was nervous. I knew that when I was locked up in detention I often ignored guest speakers, looking at them as squares. The only reason I went to the gym was to get out of my cell and see my homies that were housed in other blocks. I never paid the guest speakers any attention and a few times, I got kicked out or got in trouble for disrupting them by throwing up gang signs to my enemies.

NATURAL BORN KILLAZ

He replies, "Man, a little mêlée just happened in your old unit. Aint nothing changed! The young Crips and Bloods are in here still tryna take each other heads off."

I shake my head saying, "See, if they wouldn't have stopped the Black Panthers, there wouldn't be any Crips or Bloods."

"Yeah, I know. Have you read that article about John Wilson in the L.A. Times today? I see you got it."

Tears hit my eyes faster than the speed of light. I knew before reading the article what it was going to say. John Wilson aka Killa Black had lost his appeal and was scheduled to be executed. Crazoe had suffered the same fate. Their lives had been a tragedy within themselves gangs, drugs, and violence destroyed everything! As I write I must say, they will continue to destroy families for generations to come if we do not wake up.

Tears of anger roll down my cheeks. I think of how John responded to my letter. He advised me to never give up my mission to save the younger generation. Thoughts of how our short period of correspondence and talking to each other over the phone turned us into the best of friends now consumed my nimd. He told me to never address him as Killa Black, because he was a changed man. Or all of the times he asked me to never give up my fight to reach out to the young gang members, because if I didn't he would haunt me dead or alive.

"Terry, here they come!"

I am lost for words as I sit thinking about John, then guess who walks through the door mean muggin' and mobbing like an Origanal Crip? Dontai Jr! He is incarcerated for juvenile murder. Tameka lost control over him when Crazoe and John became worldwide headlines. Peer pressure from the gang turned him into his father all over again. And I could tell from his demeanor that most of the

TERRY WROTEN

young Crips are looking up to him, because of his father's reputation.

I immediately grab him by the arm as he enters the gym and he jerks away, "Fool, don't grab me!"

He does not know me but I know him. I get a little hostile. My old gangsta comes out. I do not like what I am seeing so I say, "Cuzz, do you know who I am?"

Dontai's whole swag changes. He now knows I'm a Crip, but it is still a mystery to him of who I am. I say, "Check this out! I'm here to speak to you and the rest of your gang brothers about gangs. I know your father and I know what just happened to him. Do you see how much pain gangs have put your mother and countless other mothers through? Tameka is a real homegirl. And cuzz, I'm here to tell you no mother wanna see her son behind bars and her husband fried in a chair!"

Dontai is thrown off. He wants to know who I am. I know too much. I do not tell him who I am, I just say, "Ask your mother who I am. And if you ever talk to Rat, he'll tell you my resume. But right now I need your help..."

~~~~~~

It's 10 o'clock in the evening and I'm finally relaxing after my long day. My talk with the juveniles at Central Juvenile Hall went well. It actually went better that I had thought. I used Dontai as the topic for my lecture. I told the story of Killa Black. Everyone in the audience walked out of the gym with tears in their eyes. I ended up telling Dontai who I was and he gave me a hug.

"Man I'm sorry! I know I be letting my father down, but I wanna change. Can you help me? You like family."

I was so elated at his response I replied, "Imma do more than help you. Imma try and get you outta here."

NATURAL BORN KILLAZ

As I relax and think about how I am going to help Dontai change and help him beat his murder case, I know that I have a hard fight ahead. Somewhere in the distance I hear the muffled sounds of gun shots and I know that somewhere out there another mother's son is lost to the streets and another mother's lost to the system. As I doze into the blissful world of sleep, I think of something John once told me penning this book...

"To be responsible is to respond to all opportunities that have been placed in front of you. I give you my story; now it's your time to give back! It's not how a man starts things, but how he ends them."

I wish for pleasant dreams and a brighter tomorrow that brings forth a new light to theBblack community. We have been killing each other for too long! It's time to change.

The past is history.....
The future is a mystery....
And today is a blessing....
Still we rise!
Terry Wroten

ACKNOWLEDGEMENTS

I'd like to thank the man up above for the many blessings I have seen thus far in my life. From being shot 6 times to standing trial for triple murder to being stabbed in race riots to being incarcerated at age 14 on a ten year bid to being a published author... I AM BLESSED.

Momma, Ms. Terrie L. Wroten, you named me after you because you knew I was a gift to this world. Hope to make you smile; knowing all the frowns I have put on your face. Love you much. And yes Im the world's biggest momma's boy. You only get one momma and I treasure mines.

Jan and Dave Weldon, my Aussie parents. Dave even though you are not here with us, you have touched many lives. Jan words can't express my gratitude for you. Love ya mum.

To my family, my aunties: Niece, Samantha, Dee, Quake and Tony. My God-pops and step-pops, Big Ant and Twin, a hard head makes a soft a** but Im still breathing. My cousins: Shanda, Kiona, Phylicia, Erica, Eric 1 &2, Aaron, Bernard, Ant Man, Day-Day 1 &2, Phillip 1 &2, Alex, Lil' Bill, Jasmine, Renesha and whoever else might skipped my mind... Love y'all. My sisters, Tee-Tee and Bre-Bre, if I could be an author, y'all could be anything y'all put y'all minds to. My brother, Anthony 'HP' Ennis, stay at it and never give up. Imma be the first to say it, you are the funniest comedian out. Hollywood here we come. Real Talk! We talked about this many a nights so make it happen captain.

NATURAL BORN KILLAZ

To the hood side of things. The 43GCs, the 42GCs, and the 48GCs. "We 50 Niggaz Deep!" My clique TLB (Tiny Loc Bastardz): my brother, Lil' Crip Time, Santana, Young Dopey, Tiny Loc, C-Dog4, Shady4, MD, B-Berry2&3, Spike, BR, Bam3, BK2 and the list goes on Love y'all. My pops in these streets, Tiki, it's been I long journey but u helped this boy become a man. And as the saying goes "If they hate, then let 'em hate and watch the money pile up." My niggaz TC, Hitman, and Neto I did it y'all. Strange aka Kenyatta, what more can I say. Can't forget about my niggaz from Harlem 30s, ECC and any other hood that got love for me. My Blood niggaz and relatives y'all know who y'all are, but a special shout out go to Juice aka B-note, Red, and Aaron Witten. "What that shit do, BLOOD!" Bandit from 60s and Godfather from Main Street, I got y'all homie. To my niggaz locked up, stay strong and sucka free! It's too many of y'all to name just COME HOME! Real Talk!!

K'wan, and my big sis (his wife) Charlotte, y'all saw the vision and walked me through some of my darkest times. Love y'all much.

And last but not least my Facebook and Twitter family. Y'all know who y'all are so get at me and much-much love... TLW